PUZZLE HOUSE

DUNCAN RALSTON

SHADOW WORK PUBLISHING

Cover art by Christian Bentulan
JMH Angelis by Joorgmoron
and Sanitarium BB by Blambot
fonts used by permission.

ISBN 978-1988819402

ALSO BY DUNCAN RALSTON

Gristle & Bone (Collection)
Salvage (Novel)
Wildfire (Novella)
Woom (Novella)
The Method (Novel)
Video Nasties (Collection)
Ebenezer (Novella)
Ghostland (Novel)
The Midwives (Novel
In Every Dark Corner (Collection)
Afterlife: Ghostland 2.0 (Novel)
Ghostland: Infinite (Novel)
Gross Out (Novel)
Skin Flicks (Collection)
Try Not to Die: at Ghostland
(Gamebook, w/ Mark Tullius)

For more, visit
www.duncanralston.com.

FOR DANIKA:
KLAATU, VERATA, NECKTIE.

CODEX

GREAT HOUSE!
FOR THE ENEMY IT IS A TRAP LYING
IN WAIT... EVEN A POWERFUL MAN
CANNOT OPEN UP ITS DOOR.

— "A HYMN TO NUNGAL"
SUMERIAN POEM, C. 2000 – 1600 B.C.E.

THE PRISONER

At the sound of the cell door clattering open, Henry Hall raised his eyes. Sunlight streaming in through the barred window above the guard's head caught the man in silhouette in the doorway. Even without seeing his face Henry could tell it was Atkins, a day shift newbie, standing with his right hand on his baton as if daring Henry to make a sudden move or say something smart just so he could pummel him. The son of a bitch had been giving Henry grief ever since he'd wound up working in the solitary confinement wing. Like he didn't already get enough grief from the other guards for what he'd done to get him put in here in the first place.

"Warden wants a word with you," Atkins said.

Henry's eyes were still adjusting to the difference in light but he stood up from the thin mattress and cracked his back. He wiped the corners of his eyes. "What does the warden want with me?"

"How the hell should I know? Move your ass, Hall."

Not wanting to give the prick any further motivation, Henry got moving and turned around at the door to his cell with his hands behind his back. He had it pretty cushy compared to guys in Gen Pop. His lawyer was able to get him a color TV, as well as paint and paintbrushes but no canvas, just a large hardcover spiral notebook. He guessed they figured he could break down the frames and do some damage with the splintered wood to himself or to others. Either way, the notepad was a decent size and thick paper, and had helped keep him from cracking up in his time spent in his small cell.

Atkins slapped on the shackles. He always put them on too tight, pinching into Henry's wrists, even when they let him out into the yard for exercise. Just another way for him to assert control.

"Get moving," Atkins said, giving Henry a single shove in the middle of his back.

Henry stumbled and righted himself. He walked at a normal pace until they reached the gate, where Atkins rapped on the bars with his baton. The lock buzzed and the gate rolled open.

Henry stepped through briskly.

The guard stationed here—his name was Chip Edwards but everyone called him Pokey for reasons unbeknownst to Henry—eyed him narrowly before looking away. Nobody was quite sure how to treat Henry since he'd shown up here. He'd murdered a cop, but he'd also been one himself, putting the motto of "protect your own" to the test with every interaction. Usually, they ignored him as much as possible, refusing even to make eye contact. When forced to, while passing other cons on janitor duty in the halls or watching over him in the library, they made a big deal about calling him "cop-killer," almost to the point of absurdity.

Not Atkins, though. Atkins had hated Henry from the second they'd stuck him in this wing, and he took every opportunity to make it known.

"Jesus, Hall, were you *crying*? You're lucky you're in solitary, the monsters out in Gen Pop'd whip up a batch of pancakes in your asshole for breakfast, lunch and dinner."

Henry ignored the jibe and kept walking. The warden's office was all the way over in C-Wing. Cushy and bright, with a view of the yard. Henry would often see Warden Jones looking down from the window during his solo exercise time, hands behind his back, puffing on a fat cigar. Wood cleaner and cigar smoke permeated the air in this spacious, sunny room. Mahogany and dust were the two most common surfaces.

"Take the shackles off," the warden said, puffing on the gnarled stub of a stogie in the brown leather chair behind his desk.

"Sir?" Atkins said.

"He won't give me any trouble." Warden Jones scowled at Henry with eyes as gray as the haze of smoke hovering around his head. "Will you, Hall?"

"No, sir, I don't intend to."

"Good." He sat the chewed-up stub in a vintage ashtray already filled with crushed cigars and piles of ash, a white ceramic one commemorating the 1971 World Champion Dallas Cowboys, while Atkins grudgingly took off the shackles. When the guard finished, he stepped back, eyeing Henry narrowly. The warden pointed to the chair opposite him at the desk and Hall sat. The brown leather was softer than the mattress in his cell. His ass cheeks hadn't felt this pampered in nearly two years.

"Leave us, would you, Atkins?"

"But, sir..."

Warden Jones didn't say a word. He didn't need to. The knitting together of his bushy black eyebrows spoke for him. Atkins gave Henry one last fuck-around-and-find-out glare before leaving the office.

"Now," the warden said, leaning forward in his chair. "Let's get down to brass tacks, shall we?"

"Okay."

Henry couldn't imagine what could've possibly gotten him summoned to the warden's office. He hadn't been in any trouble since he'd been locked up, for the simple fact that outside of the few times a day he interacted with the guards, he had no one to get in any trouble *with*. Recent appeals to shorten his fifteen-year sentence for first-degree murder had been rejected, since he'd pleaded guilty to the crime. The only thing he could think was that something had happened to Mercy. His heart began to thud in his ears at the thought of her in trouble.

"My wife—she's okay, right?"

"This isn't about your wife. Well, it is and it isn't."

"What does that mean?"

"I'm getting around to it, Hall." Jones unwrapped a fresh cigar, moistened the tip with spit, then lit it with a brass Zippo, rolling it between his fingers and puffing out small bursts of smoke until the entire tip glowed red when he sucked on it.

11

"Have a smoke, if ya like," he suggested.

Henry startled, but of course the warden knew he had smokes. Cigarettes were banned in California prisons but banning them had only made them more valuable. He'd had one a few hours ago during his yard time, which Jones would have seen. He limited himself to one a day, believing that if he smoked more he'd only crave them more often. He shook his head.

"Suit yourself," Warden Jones said, puffing away greedily. Then he slid the small stack of paper at his elbow across the desk, the text still facing him.

Henry regarded the document. It said *LAST WILL AND TESTAMENT OF* in calligraphic script, along with a name scrawled in the underlined area. A lot of legalese followed, which he couldn't make sense of upside-down. "What's this?"

"Looks like a will, doesn't it?"

"But whose will? Who is…" He struggled to decipher the signature. "…Alexis Vasiliev?"

"Alexei. That's also what I wondered, so I looked it up. Turns out he's—he *was*, excuse me—the world's foremost puzzle master, which I didn't know was a thing until I read those words just about a half hour before you stepped into my office."

Henry frowned. Outside in the yard, some guys were shouting, in some kind of scuffle. Every so often he thought it would be nice to see other faces, even if the people behind those faces wanted to kill him. Hearing that sound reminded him how lucky he was to be in solitary. As a former cop, he'd have been torn to shreds in Gen Pop. He doubted they'd even do him the honor of making him their bitch. They'd likely just treat him like a human pinata until someone stopped them or his heart did it for them.

"What does it have to do with me?"

The warden leaned forward, licked a thumb and flipped pages until he found what he was looking for. He turned the document to face Henry and pointed out Henry's full name, including both middle names, printed right under the heading *Beneficiaries*. There were five other names below his own.

"I don't even know this person."

"Well, that answers my next question. You been here, what, Hall? Almost two years?"

"Just about."

"And in those two years, you haven't gotten into any trouble. No shenanigans. In fact, most of my men, aside from Atkins out there, might go as far as to say you've been a model prisoner."

Henry remained quiet. He didn't want to give Jones any sort of ammunition to punish him should he decide Henry was being cocky.

"My point is, Hall, I think you're due some day leave."

Henry sat up straight. "Day leave, sir?"

"Says here you'll have to attend a reading of the will. Now, it was my understanding that wills don't generally *require* readings anymore, least that's how it worked when my aunt Berle died last summer. Especially when said will is sitting here right in front of us. But your inheritance, it's made quite clear, is contingent upon you showing up to this reading." Jones fixed him with his cold gray glare. "Which *I* intend to make happen."

Henry paused a moment before speaking. "What's in it for you?" he said finally.

"Get up, son." The warden eased out of his own chair. "Come stand with me at the window for a sec."

Warily, Henry pushed himself out of the comfy chair. He moved around the table casually, not wanting to do anything that might be considered a threatening movement. He knew how these things worked, how easily Jones could call Atkins back in, make it look like he was being attacked, get him beaten to within an inch of his life.

Warden Jones waved him closer. "C'mere, son."

Henry did as he was told, moving to within a foot of the man, close enough to smell his cheap aftershave and see the tangle of gray hairs in his ears. Jones draped an arm over Henry's shoulders, and though Henry felt anxious, as if the warden might turn on him at any second, he didn't attempt to move away.

"Look out there. What do you see?"

Henry looked through the window down at the yard.

Dozens of prisoners stood in various groups, mostly race-similar, lifting weights, smoking, kicking gravel, shooting hoops, while guards stood by with dour faces caught in shadow under their hat brims. In the tower stood one of the only guards in the penitentiary allowed to carry a gun. The only other was in the tower not visible from the warden's windows.

"I see a yard full of assholes, sir."

The warden laughed. "You got me there. Look closer."

While considering what sort of reply Jones might be looking for, he took a more observant look at the yard, the sort of eye he'd have given it as a detective if it were the scene of a crime. Speaking of assholes, the yard really was a shithole. The paving stones were cracked, the gravel was sparse, the grass was dry and patchy, the basketball net hung on by a hinge, the net itself torn. Even the weights looked shoddy, the benches covered in yards of duct tape. He'd never really noticed when he was led out there for his yard time. He'd just been grateful to get outside, get some air that didn't reek of cleaning products and the toilet visits of his neighbors. But would Warden Jones want to hear that? He'd always seemed to be the sort of man who prided himself on the appearance of his institution.

"It could use some repairs," Henry said cautiously.

Warden Jones pulled him in closer. "Hit the nail on the head, Hall. You ask what's in it for me?" The warden showed his teeth in a shark's grin, still clenched around the lit cigar. "Half," he said.

"Half of what, exactly?"

"Well, it says in the will that there are six beneficiaries, yourself included. I assume that's a six-way split, though I haven't had my lawyers look into the fine print as yet. Half of that would go to your wife, of course, and if the other half should find its way into the barren coffers here at the penitentiary—well, as you can see we could do heckuva lot of good with twelve-point-five million dollars."

"*Twelve-point-five...*" Henry sucked in a sharp breath, marveling at the number. It made him wonder again just who this puzzle maker Vasiliev was, and why he would've been named in the man's will. "This guy's worth one hundred and

14

fifty million dollars?"

The warden finally let him loose. "That's right, you're a math whiz. Heard Pokey mention that, I think. Regular Rain Man, he said. Yup, one hundred and fifty, at least that's what it said on the internet. I suppose some of that money could be tied up in all kinds of red tape, but that's a risk I'm willing to take."

"So, you'll just… let me out?"

Warden Jones gestured toward the chair Henry had occupied a moment ago. Henry returned to it while the warden eased back into his own. "You'll be chaperoned, let's say. The, uh, stipulations here say you'll be allowed one guest, on account of your condition. I'm sure Atkins will be more than happy to tag along."

"Atkins," Henry said. *Of all fucking people*, he thought but didn't add.

"There a problem with that?"

"No, sir. When is it happening?"

"Day after tomorrow," the warden said. "Nine a.m. sharp."

"Is it all right if I call Mercy? Let her know—"

"Your wife's been informed." The warden puffed out a plume of smoke that caught in the sunlight, swirled and eddied in the cool air from the vent above his head. "This isn't a conjugal visit, Hall. You'll go straight to the house, attend the reading, sign whatever the hell documents they need you to sign, and Atkins'll get you right on back into your cell before midnight or I'll turn his ass into a pumpkin."

Henry didn't have to spend too long considering it. It would've been nice to see Mercy without bulletproof glass between them for once. But he wasn't about to blow his opportunity to get outside these walls for the first time in nearly two years. He missed seeing civilization, seeing the hustle and grind of the city. He even missed the traffic through Boyle Heights on I-5. Sure, he'd have to deal with Atkins, but even though he'd be seeing the city through the tinted bulletproof glass of a penitentiary van, it would be worth dealing with that prick for a few hours.

"What did Mercy say?"

The warden frowned. "She said do it for Clara. That's your

daughter, is that right?"

Henry nodded, holding a wave of emotions at bay.

"You could set her up for life with this, Hall. So... what d'you say?"

"Okay," Henry agreed.

Warden Jones grinned, puffing out a celebratory cloud of smoke. "Well, okay then. Atkins, get your ass back in here," he called out.

The door opened behind them.

"Looks like the two of you are going on a road trip."

"Me... and *him*?" Atkins said in disbelief.

"That's right. Think you can handle that without fuckin it up?"

Henry could tell it took Atkins work to keep the anger from reaching his face. "Yes, sir."

"Good. Get him back to his cell."

Atkins put the shackles back on Henry but didn't dare close them too tightly in front of the warden. When he'd finished, he stepped back, allowing Henry to get ahead of him rather than give the shove he normally would have.

"One last thing, Hall," the warden said as Atkins opened the door. "If Ms. Reese does attend, get her autograph for me, would ya? My gal's a big fan."

Ten minutes later, Henry sat alone on his hard mattress staring at the wall. He thought about reading or painting, but his mind was buzzing too fast to focus. He considered watching TV but even that felt like a distraction.

Twelve-point-five million. The seemingly impossible number circled his mind. Not only would it set Mercy up for life, she could live the life of her dreams with that kind of cash. He worried she might think better of spending the next thirteen years waiting for him to get free when she could do anything she wanted. Did she really still love him that much, after what he'd done?

His gaze fell again on one of several phrases he'd found scratched into the wall when he'd first taken up residence in this six-by-nine cell: *NUNGAL WAS HERE*. He'd found himself staring at it often, at first wondering if Nungal was the name of the last poor soul stuck in this shithole of a box, then when he'd had a chance to look it up in the library, he'd wondered why someone had chosen to carve one of the names of the ancient Mesopotamian goddess of prisons and/or their version of Hell on the wall.

Had the man worshipped Nungal, or just imagined her presence to comfort himself? Whatever the reason, it had always bothered Henry enough to cover it with one of his paintings. Just knowing it was there below the rough paper was enough to trouble him some days. But when he'd returned to his cell after his meeting with the warden, he'd found the painting on the floor and the strange message staring him in the face, across from his bed.

He regarded the painting in his hands, the one that had fallen or been taken off the wall while he'd been elsewhere. It was a portrait of his daughter, based on a photo Mercy had taken when Clara was six or seven. He'd painted it from memory. Some days he forgot what she'd looked like the last time he'd seen her alive and had to rely on the single photo he'd been allowed to bring in with him. Other days he remembered all too clearly the sight of her lying on that morgue table, the back of her head a ruin of blood and skull fragments in a tangle of wavy auburn hair. Today had been one of the latter type of days, until Atkins had opened the door to his cell.

He had been crying.

He'd cried most days since Clara died.

And whether this twelve-point-five million dollars was real or not, he suspected he always would.

17

THE WIDOW

Three men dressed in black military uniforms and tactical gear chased Joy around the corner into a blind alley. Heart in her throat, she scanned the area she'd found herself in while still in mid-run. The sheer face of a brick wall blocked her escape. More walls to the left and right, housing doors with no outside handles, closed her in. She was caught.

Her gaze fell on the dumpster. It was a good five-foot jump from it to the bottom of a ladder connected to the fire escape, but she made a quick assessment and ran for it, hoping it would hold. She leapt onto the dumpster, pulled herself up to stand and jumped, reaching out for the bottom of the ladder.

She caught the first rung in both hands—she'd practiced this move countless times—and began pulling herself up.

The first mercenary ran into the alley. He spotted her and grabbed her foot before she was able to pull herself up to the next rung. She wasn't prepared for this fight. She'd just been on an undercover operation, dressed for a black-tie gala. She'd worn a Vivienne Westwood dress and heels. Now she was barefoot beneath a pair of sheer stockings. She kicked at the man's shoulder. The heels would have done more damage but were impossible to run in. The merc reared back his head and pulled harder.

Joy's fingers slipped off the rung and she fell into the puddle below in her stocking feet, dropping into a pose often called the "superhero landing," crouched with one hand resting on the ground and the other outstretched behind her back as if she were a Greek Olympian about to hurl a discus.

The first merc's partners scuttled into the alley.

Joy raised her head with a look signaling she was ready to give them hell.

The first merc came at her hard with his K-Bar knife. She stood and swung out with her right arm in one smooth, expertly practiced movement, striking his forearm with hers and deflecting the blow. He countered from a different angle and she ducked the swing, simultaneously throwing a knee up into his groin, knocking the wind out of him and sending him back several feet.

The other two men flanked her, taller than her by at least a foot. With balletic movements, she deflected their attacks. Fists swung. Boots struck out. She blocked, the blows juddering against her bones and muscle, honed by months of training. She returned their punches, elbowing the merc on the left in the chest, striking the one on the right with an uppercut.

The first recovered from his groin injury and moved in. When all three were positioned just right, equidistant to each other, Joy leapt into the air and spun. Her roundhouse missed the closest merc but he staggered backward as if he'd been struck.

The second caught her heel in the jaw. He was standing too close, in front of his mark. He uttered a muffled cry and held his face. Joy couldn't stop the spinning herself—her two stunt coordinators were still trying to stop the wire while lowering her—but fortunately Tom stepped out of the way before she could injure another colleague.

"*CUT!*" Jackson shouted behind the camera.

"I'm sorry, Leo," Joy Reese said to the stuntman she'd kicked in the face, pouting at him dramatically.

He showed her his blood-streaked teeth in a grin. "My bad, Reese. I was off my mark."

Rishi, the continuity person, stepped in quickly to take photos of Joy, the stunt actors and set.

"What the 'ell 'appened, Joy?" Jackson said, stepping onto set. Jackson Davies-Smith's accent was Mancunian, dropping his Hs and Ts. Joy liked to joke he sounded like an eighteenth-century bootblack.

Leo held up a hand smeared with blood. "I was off my mark, Jax. It's all good."

Jackson gave him a sharp look and scratched his chin stubble. "Well, let's not let that 'appen again, eh?"

Leo nodded and stalked off.

"You good?" Jackson asked, stepping in closer to speak with Joy on a personal level. He reached out to touch her shoulder, then retracted it. Joy had insisted they keep their on-set interactions professional, the optics of such things more important now than ever.

"My fucking feet are killing me," she said, rubbing the heel that had connected with Leo's face. "I think the pads are wearing out from doing that fucking jump a hundred times."

Jackson gave her a sympathetic look. "Right. We'll get costumes to put a new pair on you pronto, shall we?"

"Thanks. I just don't understand why the world's greatest secret agent wouldn't have convertible heels."

Jackson grinned. "Tell that to Manolo Blahnik, dear. I don't make the shoes." He began walking away, calling over his shoulder, "I'm merely the man behind the camera. All right, let's take five, everyone! Time for tea!"

The stunt co-ords approached Joy and began removing the wires from her harness.

"That last spin gave me a headache," she said.

Burt chuckled. "Not as bad as Leo's."

"Touché."

"Let's grab some lunch, Joy. Craft's got lobster Thermidor."

They headed toward the craft service tables together, leaving Burt's latest protégé to deal with looping up the wires. "Wow, they really stepped up their game," she said.

"That's for sure. You know, when I was starting out in the business, the films I was working on, they coulda cut their budgets in half if you ordered soup instead of the salad."

Joy grinned. "I've heard that one before, Burt."

Burt smiled back, partly obscured by his bushy gray mustache. "Hey, I'm here all week."

She and Burt Addleton had worked together on the last three action pictures she'd starred in. On the first, she'd played second-fiddle to Tom Cruise. On the second and third, she'd been top billed. This was their fourth together, a wire-fu spy drama slash action epic. Currently, she was the second highest-paid female action star in Hollywood, just below Scarlett Johansson's massive ninety-five-million-dollar payday for *Black Widow*.

They got into the chow line behind the First AD, Rishi and the Script Supervisor. Joy and Burt chatted about his grandkids, he showed pictures to Rishi and the Script Supervisor—Joy continually forgot whether she preferred Angie and Ange—who both oohed and ahhed. Joy wasn't much into children. She liked them well enough, but she'd never seen the appeal of having any of her own. It was enough for her to be a "cool aunt" to her sister's kids, who visited a couple of times a year.

Joy had just gotten her plate of lobster Thermidor, the sauce and cheese still bubbling within the two split halves of the creature. Joy had always found crustaceans to be almost otherworldly, like an Old God from some lost, ancient culture. But she had to admit they tasted wonderful, and it smelled exquisite. The company in charge of this production was well known in the business for having some of the best catering at their craft service tables.

As she followed Burt to a table, a hand grasped her arm. She startled, nearly dropping her plate. It was Jackson. He looked concerned. "Joy, can I speak with you a moment?"

"Can I eat my lunch first?"

"You'll want to hear this, dear."

She followed him to the trailers in the backlot outside the studio where the alley and several other sets had been created. A group of drivers, grips and animal wranglers—there was a tiger in this picture, caged within one of these transports—were already cleaning up from lunch, sitting on apple boxes and the steps of their trucks, smoking after-meal cigarettes, belching loudly and chuckling at likely raunchy jokes. "Hey, Miss Joy!" one of them, the tiger's owner, called over.

"Hey, Gunter," she said, waving back. She stopped in the

road and turned to Jackson. "We don't have time for a booty call if that's what this is about."

"God, Joy. If it was that I would have been a touch more subtle. Your husband—"

She narrowed her eyes to slits. They'd been separated for almost a year now. She'd just been waiting for the divorce to finalize. Any mention of him put her on edge. "What about him?"

"He's dead, Joy. He was found this morning."

"He…" She looked off. Gunter had gotten his tiger out of the cage and was walking her toward the studio. "Is this a joke?"

Jackson shook his head, his eyes downcast.

"When? What happened?"

"Heart attack, they say. Passed overnight, in his sleep."

A complicated mix of emotions washed over her: relief, sadness, guilt, each fighting for top billing. She held out her plate to Jackson, who took it, and she would've collapsed if he hadn't caught her arm. He helped her over to her trailer and they sat on the steps, Jackson one step below her.

"You all right?"

She felt woozy. Fifteen years of her life, gone in an instant. The divorce had been hanging over her head for months, not because she was worried about palimony—lord knew Alexei had plenty of his own money, though nowhere close to what she earned—but because of the tabloids. She no longer loved him, their relationship had been too tumultuous for the split to be entirely amicable, but they had still remained on mostly friendly terms. Every new article and headline about them was another dagger in the heart.

"I'll be fine," she said. "It's just… it's a lot to process."

"At least we won't have to sneak around anymore."

She flashed him a threatening glare. "This changes nothing. People *can't* know about us. Not right now. You know it wasn't just about the divorce."

He shrugged. "Fair play. Are you gonna eat this whole fing?"

Joy sighed. "Take half."

Jackson tucked in hungrily. "Look, Joy, if you need

someone to talk to—"

"We have the same shrink, Jackson."

"Right," he said, wiping his mouth with a paper napkin. "Well, you know my door's always open if you need me. In any capacity that might be."

He stopped short of winking. She didn't know what she would have done if he had. She might've hit him. Jackson knew there was bad blood between her and Alexei, but he had no idea about the complexities of their relationship. No one did, especially not the tabloids.

They *couldn't* know.

"I think I just need a few minutes to myself."

Jackson nodded, squinting off at the tiger, who leaped up to high-five her trainer. Joy was nervous about her scene with the tiger, worried it would claw her head off. But there were more important things to worry about at the moment.

"You can 'ave an 'our," Jackson said. "We'll shoot some B-roll with the tiger or somefing. All right?"

An involuntary shudder passed through her, watching the tiger and thinking of her soon-to-be ex-husband, now deceased. She'd have to work closely with the beast over the next few days, and the thought of it made her more anxious than any stunt she'd performed before. They said you could take the animal out of the jungle, but you can't take the jungle out of the animal, and those claws, those teeth… Like the old Chris Rock joke about Siegfried and Roy, *It didn't go crazy, it went tiger.*

"Thanks," she said. She grabbed the plate from him before he could start in on the other half. "Gimme that."

Then she opened the door to her trailer, stepped inside, and let it slam behind her.

Joy slapped the plate and fork down on her cluttered dressing table and sat on the edge of the sofa. She stared at the ceiling for a long moment, thinking she might cry, but she'd spent an hour in the makeup chair this morning and didn't want to repeat that. She'd made a career out of controlling her emotions down to the smallest twitch, but holding back her tears this time proved more difficult.

Instead, she stood, smoothing the waist of the Vivienne

Westwood dress, and rummaged through her purse for the burner phone. She speed-dialed the only number, waited through three rings. When the man picked up on the other end she said, "That thing you were going to do for me... it's no longer needed."

The man on the other end said nothing, but she could tell he was there. She heard his breathing, slow and steady.

"He's gone," she said, thinking she owed the man at least a little explanation for canceling the job she'd paid him a hundred grand to do. "I'm free."

"What about the money?" the man said.

"It's yours. Keep it."

He smacked his lips, as if in thought. "Wipe the phone and throw it away. Forget this number."

With that, the call disconnected. Joy snapped off the back cover of the flip phone, removed the SIM card, wiped the data, and returned the phone to her purse. She made a note to dump the phone and SIM in different areas on her way back to her house in Laughlin Park when shooting wrapped for the day.

The phone number she'd already forgotten.

THE HEALER

Take a deep breath and hold it," the automated voice said.

"Take a deep breath and hold it," Oscar Evans repeated, mocking the voice. He kept his hands above his head and did as instructed. The contrast dye pumped through his veins and the CT scanner began gliding up his midsection, the X-ray tube spinning, blasting beams of electromagnetic energy throughout his body. Iodine burned like acid through his circulatory system.

When the machine stopped rotating and returned to its default position, the technician entered the room. She removed the lead pad from his groin and the IV from his wrist.

"That wasn't so bad, was it?"

Oscar disagreed but didn't respond. He'd ordered hundreds of these tests for his patients, but this was the first time he'd undergone it himself. The burning sensation of the iodine had dissipated but the pinch of the needle in his wrist still stung as the tech applied gauze and tape to the injection site.

"Apply pressure for at least a minute," she said.

Oscar grinned. "I've done a few of these in my time."

The tech smiled in return. "Of course, Doctor."

He stood, feeling slightly woozy. The gown had come open in the front and he tied it back up awkwardly while holding the bandage against his skin.

"You should get the results in a few days."

As an epidemiologist who dealt with deadly diagnoses more often than he'd prefer, Oscar was already relatively certain he knew what the results would show, just not how bad it was. He'd been pissing streaks of blood for weeks. At first, he'd been able to convince himself it was just inflammation from having a few too many on the weekends with his friends. When the first of the sharp bouts of pain came he assumed ureter stones, but the pain hadn't been spasmodic and he'd had no trouble urinating. In fact, he'd been pissing a lot more than normal. And the pain hadn't limited itself to burning in his abdomen and urinary tract, it had spread along his lower back in throbbing waves.

He realized then it was time to consider it might be cancer and get himself an appointment right away.

Dr. Alan Horowitz specialized in urology, and had graduated from the same year and class as Oscar. He'd managed to squeeze Oscar in the very next day, ordering what he'd called "the whole shebang": urine cytology, CT scan and a follow-up to discuss the results.

Oscar had pissed into a cup and handed it to Marlene, Alan's nurse, before leaving work for the day. He'd been able to book the CT scan the following Monday. Between then and now, Alan had called him to let him know the urinalysis had shown cancer cells.

"Now that doesn't mean we can't get you free and clear," he said. "We still don't know how aggressive it is, nor where it's located."

His phone rang as he was putting his clothes back on in the cramped changing room just outside the radiology clinic. Oscar pumped hand sanitizer into his palm and rubbed his hands quickly together in concentric circles until the alcohol evaporated before picking it up.

"Hello?" he said.

"Dr. Evans," a flat voice replied. "Dr. Oscar Evans."

His suspicions rose but he maintained his calm tone. "This is him."

"Dr. Evans, my name is Trent Foxworth. I'm a legal representative for Alexei Vasiliev."

"I'm sorry—who?"

"My client has named you as a beneficiary in his will. I'm

26

just going through the names and numbers at the moment informing you all."

"Why would I be named in the will of a man I've never heard of until just now?"

"You'd be surprised how many times I've heard that today. Irregardless—"

"Regardless," Oscar corrected him.

"*Regardless*," the attorney said, "you've been named and your presence is required to receive your bequest."

"My bequest. Is this a joke? I mean is this some kind of hidden camera thing?"

"I assure you, Dr. Evans, this is no joke. Mr. Vasiliev was something of a philanthropist. He liked to give. And apparently, he'd like to give some of his, some might say, *vast* fortune to you."

"I'm not a charity case, Mr...."

"Please. Call me Trent."

"I don't *need* money, Trent," he said, thinking that with no spouse and no children and maybe six months to a year to live if he didn't follow through with treatment, money was the last thing he needed. What he needed was *time*.

"Regardless, Mr. Vasiliev has chosen you as one of six beneficiaries to his estate. If you don't show up... well, I suppose the remaining beneficiaries will find themselves that much richer."

"Who are the others? Strangers, too?"

"You'll receive a physical document in the mail today or tomorrow. As I said, I'm just—"

"Going through the name and numbers," Oscar said, repeating back his words.

"Exactly. *Regardless*, I do hope to see you there."

"When is it? The reading?"

"In three days, Dr. Evans. Thank you for your time."

The call disconnected.

Oscar regarded the screen—the caller ID showed FOXWORTH & CO. ATTORNEYS, not the Unknown Caller he expected to see—then slipped the phone back into the right front pocket of his pants and put on his lab coat.

He ate lunch before heading back to the lab, a thick Reuben sandwich with wedge-cut fries. His colleagues often wondered where he stored all the extra fat and carbs. In truth, Oscar didn't know himself. He'd always had a high metabolism. He typically had a single BM in the morning, roughly ten minutes after his first coffee. He worked out regularly but not excessively, just enough to stay fit. He didn't smoke and he only drank on the weekend.

He supposed he'd always just been lucky.

Until now.

Right, he thought. *Until now. Except the same week you find out you've got cancer suddenly you're in some rich guy's will. How rich is this guy, anyway?*

Oscar left the changing room and deposited the gowns into the bin. In the elevator back to his office, he looked up this Alexei Vasiliev. As the elevator rose, Oscar felt his heart drop when he read the man's net worth. A guy could do a lot of good with that much money, dependents or not. He could give it all to some charity. Habitat for Humanity or Doctors Without Borders. Something like that.

How someone could make that amount of money as a "puzzle maker," even the "world's foremost," was beyond Oscar's imagination. He'd read that Vasiliev made "complicated and unique" games, mazes and puzzles for the rich and famous. Some of them, it said, were "larger than life."

In the results were photos of seemingly impossible mazes made from hedges and stone, as well as "mechanical" puzzles, carved from wood or fashioned from brass with cogs and gears that looked like a set piece from Charlie Chaplin's *Modern Times*, some small enough to fit in the palm of a hand, others as large as the one currently taking up almost the entire lobby of the Museum of Natural History in Buffalo. He'd also created puzzles for notable board game manufacturers and escape room companies. It said he was one of only two people in the world to hold a degree in Enigmatology from Indiana University, the study of puzzles.

Oscar was a bit of an art buff and was surprised he hadn't heard of Vasiliev sooner, though he supposed the art of puzzlemaking was a very different world. The pieces he saw as he flipped through the photos were clearly works of staggering creative genius, but not in the same sense as a da Vinci or Michelangelo.

The elevator doors opened and Oscar stepped out. As he walked down the hall to his office he was doubled over by a sharp pain in his bladder and had to pause, grasping his side.

"Everything okay, Dr. Evans?"

He looked up to see Janessa, a young technician from the lab. She seemed harried, and was likely heading off to grab a quick lunch before returning to continue analyzing the blood and tissue samples they'd collected this morning from some patients in an elderly care home in Sherman Oaks.

He stood abruptly, gritting his teeth against the pain so he wouldn't wince. Nobody knew about his medical issues, aside from Alan and Alan's nurse, and now potentially Julie in the radiology clinic. He wanted to keep it that way, at least until he got the results.

"I'm fine," he said with a slightly noticeable groan. "My eyes were bigger than my stomach. Any data on those samples yet?"

"Nothing yet. I *think* it could be some sort of viral infection, judging by the PCR and negative stain EM," she said hesitantly. "But I don't want to jump to conclusions."

"Good. Wait on those HA results."

"You think we have time?" she asked anxiously.

"Janessa, it's only half a dozen patients. That hardly qualifies as an outbreak, does it? It's a cluster."

She sighed and nodded. "Okay. Want anything from the caf?"

"I'm good, thanks. Just finished one of their gigantic Reuben and fries. Hence the bubble gut," he said, patting his stomach.

She gave him a studious look. "You are looking a little pale, though. Hope it's not a bug."

"I'll be fine," he said with a tight smile. "Get some lunch. And try not to worry. We'll figure this out. Okay?"

She nodded again. "Okay. Thank you, Doctor."

"Like I said, you can call me Oscar outside the lab."

She smiled. "Thank you, Oscar."

Oscar watched her hurry off toward the elevators, shaking his head. The pain had dissipated, but now he had to piss again. It'd been an especially painful bout, and made him worry the cancer was much further along than he'd hoped. The pains seemed to be getting worse by the day.

He went into the public washroom, skipped the urinal and went directly to a stall. Anxiety over the impending pain made it difficult to start, and when he did finally get going the burn was more painful than he'd expected. He let out a groan that made the guy at the urinals immediately flush and leave without washing his hands. He gripped his sides to keep from crying out again and let the blood-streaked urine splash against the bowl.

When the last of it trickled out, he sighed heavily, wiped— the shock of seeing blood on the tip of his penis had vanished months ago—and flushed, then washed his hands thoroughly.

As he dried his hands and left the bathroom he turned over the conversation with the lawyer in his mind. On the one hand, if he managed to survive the cancer he could do a lot of good with that money. Even if he didn't survive, he could use it to start some kind of charitable foundation. Turn something terrible into something good. His entire life he'd fought to make his mark in this world, to leave something of meaning behind. A legacy.

The last thing on his mind as he returned to the lab was the care home viral cluster. He was confident they'd be able to solve it swiftly and quietly, and a beneficial new drug would be on the market in months rather than the years they would've otherwise wasted on clinical trials.

At least that was what he convinced himself of to make his predicament feel like a complex moral decision rather than the blackmail it was.

THE HOUSE

It's a lot smaller than I thought it would be," came a voice behind Joy, startling her from what had been a mostly unpleasant stream of memories.

She turned to see a Hispanic man slightly shorter than herself and maybe a decade older, with a receding hairline and a double chin, yet otherwise slim with broad shoulders. His awkward smile faltered. "You look familiar," he said. "Don't I know you?"

She got this often, people mistaking her for someone they knew before they'd clue in to where they'd seen her before. Usually, it took a few seconds. Sometimes they'd remember as they were walking away.

The man squinted at her a moment longer, the morning sun in his eyes, adjusted the small backpack he held over one shoulder—Joy heard a rattle of plastic, possibly pills of some sort—then stepped up onto the sidewalk, closing their distance and gap in height. "I'm Oscar," he said. "Dr. Oscar Evans."

"Joy Reese," she said.

They shook hands. It wasn't until they'd broken contact that his face lit up with recognition, and then it all came pouring out in one long, run-on sentence, the way it often did. Once they recognized her everyone, even doctors and astronauts, suddenly turned into gushing fanboys and girls.

"Oh, wow, Miss Reese, I'm a big, big-big fan, I love the one, you know the one, where you fight all those giant centipedes, that one's my favorite."

She smiled patiently. It was one of her least favorite films and most physically demanding roles. "*100 Freaking Legs*. That's my favorite, too."

"It's such an honor. I had no idea you were going to be here—wait, did you know Mister..." It was obvious he didn't remember Alexei's name. "...the deceased?" he finished with a slightly embarrassed clearing of his throat.

"Alexei's my husband. *Was* my husband."

"Oh, I... um... I'm sorry for your loss, Miss Reese. *Missus* Reese?"

"Joy is fine," she said. "And thank you." She didn't think it was important to involve this stranger in her love life, informing him of their irreconcilable differences and impending divorce. "He was a good man."

The words spilled out of her before she'd had a chance to think about them. Had he been good? He had been once, she supposed. When they'd first been courting. After the wedding, he'd changed. It had been as if he'd been hiding a secret double life the entire time. And when she'd come home early three years ago from a week of shooting in Milan, caught him with those men in the basement...

She shook her head. The memory was still somewhat hazy and the sudden appearance of the sun's reflection on the broken windows of the abandoned factory across the street brought a bright stab of pain with it, the beginning of a migraine. She reached into her purse and took out her Bvlgari sunglasses, flicked them open, and slipped them onto her face, darkening the world by degrees.

"You lived here?" the man—Oscar—asked.

"For a time. I was away a lot. Shooting."

"Of course. Well, I suppose we must be the first to arrive. Unless everyone else came by taxi."

Oscar's car, a gray Model X Tesla, was parked half a block down from the house, near the foot of the plywood fence surrounding the factory and the new sign placed in front of it. She'd arrived about ten minutes prior by Uber Lux and had sauntered down to the end of the fence to read the sign, in no rush to reenter the house in which she'd spent much of the last few years in matrimonial misery. Unsurprisingly, it'd been a notice for a condo development.

She turned to regard the house she'd shared with a man she'd apparently barely known for the past fifteen years, save the last nine or ten months since they'd been separated. It looked the same as the last time she'd been here, aside from some strange structural changes she couldn't quite understand. The house had always been the sort of boxy modern style favored by developers with no imagination, but now the divisions between the floors and rooms were visible from the outside, with what looked like large rivets on each side of the divide. It almost looked like he'd turned the house into a giant Rubik's cube of tinted glass and smooth stucco.

She was just about to ask Oscar what he thought about it when a white van emerged from behind the construction fence at the far end of the street. It drove slowly up the middle of the road and passed the fence gate, continuing toward the house.

As it neared she saw the windows were tinted, and the words stenciled on the side of the van became visible: CALIFORNIA DEPARTMENT OF CORRECTIONS.

"Is that…?" Oscar said.

"It is," she replied.

"Is it coming here?"

She didn't need to answer this, as the van slowed further and came to a jarring, brake pad-squeaking halt about ten feet from the walkway where they stood. She noticed movement in the driver seat, obscured by the dark glass. A moment later the driver door opened and a lanky guy dressed in a pressed navy-blue polo and pleated gray slacks stepped out, the sun winking off his black Oakleys. His crewcut was law enforcement chic for the late-'90s. The polo was tucked into the slacks and several things hung from his black tactical belt: baton, holstered handgun, Taser, Maglite, walkie-talkie and small leather pouch, closed.

Another corrections officer, a short burly woman, stepped out from the passenger seat dressed similarly, though she wore no sunglasses and kept her greasy black hair in a ponytail using a scrunchie. She leaned into the cab and emerged holding a 12-gauge shotgun in both hands. She racked it, then lumbered toward the back of the van, where she stood scowling as the male officer opened the doors.

After a moment another man became visible, stepping out from the back, dressed in an orange prison uniform. He had disheveled hair and a gaunt, haunted look to his pallid, scruffy face. He squinted up at the sky as if he hadn't seen it for years, a smile rising to accompany the haunted expression in his dark eyes.

"Here comes trouble," Oscar muttered.

Joy and Alexei had done their wills together early on in their marriage, including one another and close family members—Joy had chosen her little sister Lara to receive the bulk of what wouldn't go to Alexei, who'd bequeathed his own to his now deceased mother—as well as donations to various charities. She could only assume he'd changed his will, as she had herself, after the separation. But she couldn't imagine Alexei being friends with a convicted criminal, and it was even more unlikely that he'd added someone who was still incarcerated. Whoever this man was, Joy had never seen him before.

The prisoner, hands and feet shackled, looked up at her, their eyes locking for a moment. The haunted look on his face softened slightly and Joy looked away quickly, down at her feet. She'd long ago trained herself to maintain eye contact, pushing past the shyness of her youth in order to excel at her chosen career. She'd held the gaze of many people who could've been deranged fans or sex fiends, but she'd never met a prisoner in person before. She didn't know if he was a thief, a rapist, a murderer or worse. He could've been all three.

The guards led him toward the house, chains clanging, toward Joy and Oscar standing in the walkway. Oscar took a single nervous step back, as if hoping Joy would protect him if the prisoner decided to try to use him as a human shield. The female guard's eyes darted every which way as they walked, looking for signs of trouble. When they got closer, Joy saw a flash of recognition in the woman's eyes, but the scowl quickly returned and she continued her search for potential threats.

"You're here for the will?" Oscar said, his voice small.

"Affirmative," the male corrections officer said. The name badge on his lapel said ATKINS. The woman's said MOORE.

Oscar cleared his throat. "Does the... prisoner... *know* the deceased?"

Atkins's eyes narrowed. "What kind of question is—?"

"No," the man interrupted. His voice was soft, that of a broken man. "I've never met him before."

The guards gave him the evil eye, before Moore resumed scanning the area. Atkins pushed the prisoner forward. The chains rattled as he stumbled two steps closer to Joy and Oscar. This time Oscar remained in place, a step behind her.

"That makes two of us," he said. "I don't know him, either." He held up a hand. "I'm Oscar. Dr. Oscar Evans."

"Henry," the man said, then looked down at his chains.

"You probably recognize our third," Oscar said.

The prisoner, Henry, regarded her again. No longer sensing him as a threat—or whatever instinct had caused her to look away from him the first time—Joy held his gaze. The haunted look remained. She saw no recognition in his face.

"I'm sorry, should I?"

"I guess you don't get to watch a lot of movies in the, uh..." Oscar cleared his throat and glanced at his watch. "Well," he said, clapping his hands below the waist. "Just about time, I guess. We should probably..." He shrugged and looked back at the house. "Should you go first?" he asked Atkins. "Is that...?"

Without a word, Atkins again pushed Henry forward, shackles jingling as the prisoner shuffled to the walkway. Moore stayed on the sidewalk, shotgun gripped against her round midsection, her dark eyes forever searching for trouble.

Joy and Oscar stepped aside to allow the men to pass between them. She waited for the two to reach the front door, then took up behind Oscar. Many memories, very few of them good, awaited her inside. If not for the will, she would've been happy to never return.

Atkins opened the door, scanned the interior, then pulled Henry in by the wrist chains. Oscar ascended the first two steps, turned back with an expectant look to see if Joy was following, then entered.

35

Joy took one last look at the outside world, something that seemed suddenly important to do, as if stepping back inside this house would fundamentally change her in some way. The sun was still shining high above her. Sparrows chirped in a nearby sycamore. The factory, its windows and doors barred by giant sheets of plywood, still imposed its shadow over the only house to ever exist on Trap Street. The street itself had at first existed only on maps, the names Trap Street and Paper Street often interchangeable, a way for mapmakers to spot copycats. It was decades later, when urban sprawl and density required the street to be made, that the fictitious street became reality. The factory came first in the mid-1930s, manufacturing cheap pedal cars, as well as department store mannequins, and Kewpie doll and Buck Rogers knockoffs. The house was built across the street for the dollmakers, a husband and wife, though only bits of the original structure remained in Alexei's modernist monstrosity, just the bare bones.

Joy glanced at Moore, who caught her eye for a moment before resuming her endless search. It struck Joy as strange that she'd wait out here with the only shotgun when the prisoner would be inside the house with at least three civilians, considering an attorney or executor would likely be present for the reading. And despite his meek appearance, Henry was clearly a dangerous man.

If he's as dangerous as they think, she thought, *at least the other guard is armed.*

The thought failed to comfort her, though. For some reason, she felt more concerned about the armed guard than his unarmed prisoner.

It's the eyes. Something about him looks... off.

Thinking this, she ascended the final step to her old home, stepped inside, and shut the door behind them.

The first thing she noticed was the once-grand foyer had been made a great deal smaller since she'd last been here, now restricted to what appeared to be a Japanese *genkan*-style entrance about the size of a typical mudroom. The second was the *thunk* of what sounded like an automated lock on the front door, another new installation.

36

As she turned to reach for the door handle—which she quickly discovered wasn't there—a voice she recognized arose behind her, sending a fearful prickle up her spine.

It can't be, she thought. *It's not possible.*

"Welcome, beneficiaries," Alexei Vasiliev said, the voice causing Joy to turn and face her dead husband on the TV monitor beside the inner door. "Welcome to my home. Welcome to Puzzle House."

THE TRAP

W elcome to Puzzle House," the man said from the wide flatscreen television beside the inner door. He spoke with a thick Eastern European accent, one corner of his lips rising in a smirk. He was well lit but surrounded by darkness, his tan skin, Caesar haircut and heavy brow ridge a stark contrast to the black backdrop.

Oscar's gaze lowered from the man on the screen to the blown-up photo of him on a gold-painted altar. Beneath it was a display of yellow-petaled flowers, among which stood a small upright tablet with some form of Asian writing on it. Judging by the style of the room itself, with its wooden joists and ceiling beams, and the painted white walls and ceiling, floor mats and a shoji screen door, he supposed it was likely Japanese. The door had no handle and didn't look as if it could slide one way or the other. On the other side of it stood a headstone with the names ALEXEI FYODOR VASILIEV and JOY REESE carved horizontally into its face. Joy's name was painted red.

"Hello, Joy, my darling," the dead man said. "At least, I hope you've decided to join us?"

"The door's locked," Joy said behind them. Oscar turned to see concern on her face. *Genuine* concern, not something from one of her characters in a movie.

"What is this?" Atkins growled. He shot an accusatory glare at Joy, grabbed Henry by the wrist chains and yanked him toward the door, then reached for a handle that wasn't there. When his hand came back empty, he muttered, "What the fuck?" He whipped his head back to face the screen. "Open the goddamn door!"

"Relax, please," Vasiliev said, as if he could hear them. But of course, the man was dead—or was *supposed* to be dead. Oscar suddenly felt a pervasive external fear for his life for the first time since he'd pissed blood. He was supposed to die from cancer. At home. *In bed*. Not at the hands of some stranger in a dead man's home.

"Allow me a moment to explain, if you will. In life I was… what you might call a *peculiar* individual, as my lovely widow Joy I'm certain will attest to. As such, this will not be your typical reading of the will. This is a game, created by myself, specifically for you. The winners will receive all of my assets, liquid and fixed, including the house in which you stand at this very moment."

"I didn't sign up for any goddamn game," Atkins said. "Let us the hell out of here!"

"You have the choice to stay or leave," the dead man said, again as if anticipating what might be spoken in the room. "You're not being held here against your will, so to speak." The smile he gave the camera looked forced to Oscar. "Once you solve this first of six puzzles, you will be permitted to continue or leave—to *escape*, if you prefer the term—but please know that if you leave, you forfeit any chance you have of winning my estate, valued at over one-hundred and fifty-million dollars, for you and the other participants. In the event you forfeit, my assets will be liquidated and any and all moneys will be bequeathed to Infiniti Enterprises." Again, the faked smile. "Good luck to you all."

The screen went black for a moment before the words MAKE YOURSELVES AT HOME appeared in the same calligraphic font as the memorial.

The three beneficiaries and their uninvited fourth regarded one another. Eventually the three men's gazes fell upon Joy. She shrugged up her shoulders.

"What? I don't know anything about this."

"He's your ex-husband," Oscar said. "What kind of tricks does he have up his sleeve?"

"Honestly? I wouldn't put anything past him."

"He said it's a puzzle, right?" Henry said, his brow furrowed in thought. "We solve it, we can leave. So let's solve it."

"Shut the hell up, Hall." Atkins yanked Henry forward again. Oscar stepped aside as the guard began feeling with his free hand along the seam of shoji screen door. "There's gotta be some kind of mechanism…"

Joy said, "It won't work like that. My hus—Alexei. He made escape rooms as part of his living."

Atkins began trying to get his fingers between the door and the jam. "Help me get this door open, Hall."

"Don't bother," Joy said. "The only way to open the door is to solve his puzzle. Trust me. He once locked me in a basement room for six hours with nothing but a bottle of water and a compass. These puzzles are complex, but the solution would always be staring you right in the face."

With this, she turned to face the screen again. Oscar followed her gaze. The words MAKE YOURSELVES AT HOME remained there, an odd message to beneficiaries of a will, Oscar considered, especially when two-thirds were strangers to the deceased.

"You lived here," Henry said. "Is there anything out of place?"

"*Everything's* out of place. This used to be the grand foyer. You'd walk in to a beautiful crystal chandelier and a winding double staircase, right there in front of us. He must've had this room built specifically for the game."

Atkins groaned as his fingers slipped off the edge of the door again. "Goddammit, Hall, give me a hand."

"I'm telling you, this room is an impenetrable box," Joy said, loud enough that Atkins finally stopped working on the door. "We are not getting out of here until we solve his puzzle."

Atkins stepped away from the door finally, gritting his teeth, and punched the photograph on the stand. It bent against his fist and fell facedown at Henry's feet, knocking over the wreath, causing a spray of tiny yellow petals to scatter across the polished stone floor. "Fuck this. I knew I shoulda told the warden to take a flying fucking leap. This is *your* fault, Hall."

He jabbed a finger into Henry's chest. Henry looked at his feet, not willing to stand up for himself.

"Leave him alone," Joy said.

Atkins turned to her with a snarl. "Well, how about you, huh? He's your husband, ex—whatever. Got any fucking bright ideas about how to get out of here?"

"You catch more flies with honey," Oscar muttered. He couldn't help himself, and immediately regretted having spoken it aloud.

"What?" Atkins snapped, rounding on him with fury in his eyes. "*What did you say?*"

Oscar cringed. He wouldn't let death and disease slow him down, but confrontation terrified him. "I... I said..."

Fortunately, Joy stepped between them before he had to humble himself any further. "All right, just calm down and let me think, *please*," she said.

Atkins's eye bugged out at this. Then he said, "Wait a minute, wait a minute..." He reached for the walkie-talkie on his belt, pulled it off and thumbed the Transmit button. "Moore, this is Atkins, I need assistance, over." He waited, hearing only static. "*Moore, this is Atkins, I need assistance, over,*" he said more persistently, white-knuckle gripping the walkie.

Nothing. He lowered his arm in defeat. "What the fuck? What the fucking *fuck*?"

Joy pulled her cell phone out of her bag. "He's probably built some kind of radio signal dampener into the walls."

"Like a Faraday cage?" Oscar asked.

"Sure. I guess." She looked at the phone screen, then held it up for the others to see. Oscar took out his reading glasses and held them against his nose. The phone had no signal.

"Great," Atkins mumbled, attaching the walkie back to his belt. "Just fucking great. Now what?"

"Now, we play his game," Joy said. "And then we get the fuck out of here."

"Wait," Henry said. "You want to *leave*? There's a hundred million dollars on the table here—"

"I don't need his money," Joy said.

"Well, that's real nice for you but some of us have

41

obligations."

"Didn't you hear what I said?" Joy's voice rose to a level of frustration Oscar knew well from the *Arrowheart* film series, where she'd played swashbuckling treasure hunter Helen Arrowheart. "He left me locked in a room with *only a bottle of water* for *six fucking hours*."

"Lady," Henry said, giving her a sidelong look, "I've been locked in a room for nearly *two years* with *zero* chance of escape. I could do six hours standing on my head. And you *didn't* just have a bottle of water, he gave you a compass. I'm betting that compass was the key to you getting out of there, wasn't it?"

Joy clenched her jaw, then nodded.

"So the answer is staring us in the face, like you said. We solve one puzzle, we can solve the rest of em. They can't be that hard. How did the compass work?"

"I, um... I had to use the magnet inside the compass to flick a hidden switch in the wall."

"Okay, but I bet there were red herrings, right? Maybe a map on the wall, things like that?"

She nodded again. "A map, a sailboat in a bottle, an odometer..."

"Red herrings," Henry said.

"What are you getting at, Hall?" Atkins grunted.

"It won't be the most obvious answer, but it *will* be, when you break it down. Occam's razor."

"So... what types of things are we looking for?" Oscar asked. The only things he noticed in the room, other than what he'd already noted, were a side table with a coffee machine and a stack of Styrofoam cups, a bowl of sugar and a dish of creamers. It made him think of an AA meeting in a dojo.

"Well, first of all, there's no handles or keyholes on either of the doors. That means they're probably magnetic, like the compass lock. So, we have to find a way to trigger the mechanism and open the doors."

Standing closest to the front door, Joy flicked a switch on the wall and the lights went out, plunging them into absolute darkness.

"Hey, come on!" Atkins grunted.

She flicked the light back on, shrugging apologetically. "Had to try."

Atkins was still scowling. "What about the coat rack? Pull on the hooks."

Joy pulled each one successively. None of them moved or made a sound. She pointed at the wreath on the floor. "Alexei hated yellow flowers." The others turned to her, and she shrugged again. "Maybe there's a magnetic key hidden in it? Like a card?"

"Pick em up," Atkins said to Oscar.

"Why me?"

"Because you're closest and I don't trust this prick for a second."

Oscar shook his head and bent to pick up the flowers. In all the commotion his ailment had slipped his mind, but a stinging reminder struck him in the abdomen and back as he grabbed the flowers by the wire frame. He winced and gripped his side, holding out the wreath to Atkins. The guard snatched it from him, shaking loose a spray of yellow petals, and started rooting through it while Oscar breathed through the pain.

"Bad back?" Joy asked.

"I'll be fine, thank you," he said. *Just as long as there's a bathroom in this place*, he thought but didn't add.

"There's nothing," Atkins said, the flowers virtually picked clean, hundreds of petals and bits of stamen scattered around his feet. He threw the wire frame. It bounced across the floor and landed against the shoe mat.

"Now what?" Oscar asked. "Unless anyone can read Japanese…?"

Henry was looking at the screen. "Make yourselves at home," he muttered to himself. For a moment his face went blank. Then his eyes went wide. "What's the first thing you do when you make yourself at home? Particularly in Japan."

"You take off your shoes," Joy said.

"Do me a favor. Step on that mat, would you?"

Joy approached it. She reached out one long leg and pushed down with the toe of her high-heeled shoe.

The flat part of the mat lowered against the pressure of her foot, leaving the raised rubber rim at floor level.

Joy stepped back quickly, scanning the room like Helen Arrowheart might have for booby traps.

"Why did you stop?" Henry asked.

"Because I know my ex. And if he'd let me starve to death in a locked room when he was alive, I wouldn't put it past him to shock me or worse now that he's dead."

Oscar watched Henry consider it, then nod slowly. "All right, that's a good point. Take off your shoes and put them on the mat, will you do that?"

She gave him an anxious look.

"Then I'll do it. You'll have to take them off for me." He turned to Atkins. "Is that okay?"

Atkins narrowed his eyes a moment, then grunted an affirmative and gripped the handle of his baton. "You make one fucking move, Hall…"

Joy approached Henry cautiously. Standing face to face, she held his gaze much longer than she needed to, until Henry gave her a tight smile. Then she lowered to a crouch as he raised his right foot. She removed the orange sneaker, exposing his dirty white sock, and placed the shoe on the floor beside his foot. They did the same for the left.

She stood up holding both shoes. Henry took them from her. Atkins moved him to the door. Henry bent at the knees and placed the shoes carefully on the mat.

Nothing happened.

"It needs more weight. We need to put all of our shoes down."

Joy raised her right foot behind her and unstrapped the shoe. Oscar crouched with a sharp wince and took off his loafers one by one. He stood again and waited while Joy handed her heels to Henry. Henry placed them both on the mat. It moved perceptibly but otherwise nothing happened.

Atkins saw this and grunted. He lifted one foot to his knee and began fiddling with the laces.

"Not you," Henry said. "It's just supposed to be the three of us here."

44

Oscar handed his shoes to Henry while Atkins relaced his boots with a sneer and a shake of his head.

Henry placed the shoes on the mat. It lowered another imperceptible degree and immediately both doors, inner and outer, made loud clunks like the sound of magnetic locks disengaging. They came open several inches at once, sunshine spilling in through the front door.

"Congratulations," came Vasiliev's voice from the television. He was smiling that same fake-looking smile against the same black backdrop. "You've solved the first puzzle faster than any other group. That wasn't so hard, was it? They will get more difficult from here on, I assure you. But I think you can handle a little tougher, can't you?"

Joy ignored her deceased husband and opened the door all the way, shading her eyes as she stepped outside. The guard with the shotgun still stood at the foot of the walkway. She gave them all a perplexed look.

"You good, Atkins?"

"Yeah," he said, squinting out at her. "Everything's peachy keen, Moore. We're leaving."

"Atkins," Henry said.

"*We're leaving*," the guard said again, more forcefully.

"Warden Jones sent me here to collect that money. He *expects* that money. What do you think he'll do if we go back with nothing?"

"I don't give a shit what he does to you—"

"Not me, Atkins. *You*. He'll put you on the worst rotation on the meanest cell block. No more cushy rounds in protective custody. They'll stick you in Gen Pop. Throw you in with the rapists and human traffickers and men who butchered their own families with machetes."

"He'll throw *you* in Gen Pop."

"Maybe. The difference is, I don't give two shits if I live or die."

Oscar was captivated by the exchange, the sort of macho tete-a-tete he'd only ever seen on TV shows and witnessed briefly on public transit before quickly scuttling off to the next subway car. And he *believed* Henry's admission. As someone who'd made his own peace with death, Oscar saw a similar look each day in the mirror.

Atkins was a different beast. Oscar still couldn't get a read on him. Something about the man wasn't quite as it seemed, he knew that much just from observing him in the few minutes they'd spent inside this room. It was like every reaction had to be weighed and considered for several moments, even when he was acting out in seemingly spontaneous violence.

Finally, Atkins's eyes narrowed to slits. "Shit," he said. He grabbed the wrist chains and yanked Henry out of the sunlight, back inside the room.

Standing outside in her stocking feet, Joy looked in at the others with disbelief. "You're going back in?" She caught Oscar's eye. "Are you *kidding* me?"

Oscar shrugged. "It was kind of fun, don't you think? And nothing bad happened. I don't need the money either, but think of the good we could do with it if we won."

"People don't just make *contests* out of their wills. I don't even think it's legal."

"But if it is…" He shrugged and turned to Henry. The prisoner nodded.

"You heard what he said, it needs to be all of us," Henry said, giving Joy a pleading look. "I know you don't know me, you don't owe me anything. But I need this. My wife needs this. My…" He stopped himself, his sharp, stubbled Adam's apple bobbing, swallowing what appeared to be a profound sadness. "*Please*."

"What if we do this and there's no money?"

Oscar hadn't considered that, and judging by Henry's rapid blinks, he hadn't either. "Then you spent an afternoon at a very elaborate escape room, and I get to go back to a living Hell."

"Should I radio in?" Moore asked from the curb.

"Give us a minute," Atkins barked back.

Joy looked from one stranger to the other, searching for something in their faces. When her gaze finally settled on Oscar, he cocked his head and held up his hands as if to ask *What's the worst that could happen?*

"Step down on the mat first," she said to Henry.

Henry shuffled over as far as Atkins would allow. He pressed the toes of his dirty right sock against the mat and pushed down hard until it clicked. The front door began to close immediately. He stepped off quickly.

"See? No booby traps. Nothing to be afraid of."

Oscar recognized the look of annoyed resignation Joy gave Henry from her early comedy films. "Fine. But if I have to say I told you so..."

She stepped back inside and collected her shoes from the mat. As she balanced on one foot to put them on, the front door shut behind her.

"Give us two hours, Moore," Atkins called out through the narrowing gap. "If you don't hear from me by then, call the warden."

Oscar saw a flash of concern in the woman's eyes as the door closed the final few inches. Then it thudded shut, and the magnetic lock engaged, sealing them into the house once more.

Only then did it occur to him what had been bothering him since Henry had set his shoes on the mat, causing it to sink the correct amount to open the doors. "Wait a second. How did they know how much each of our shoes would weigh?"

"They didn't," Henry said.

He and Joy looked up toward the high right corner of the room. Atkins and Oscar followed their gazes, both of them spotting the small, dark camera bubble.

"Someone is watching us," Henry said.

They all stood looking at the camera, contemplating this for a silent moment.

"Well," Oscar said finally, only to dispel the feeling of dread that had suddenly overcome him. "I guess we better get started."

He opened the inner door wide enough to step through, and what he saw made his eyes widen in surprise. Here was the grand foyer Joy had described: everything opulent white and gold and black and deep red, a crystal chandelier high above, casting its warm glow on the two curved wooden staircases with Persian carpet runners and the dark Baroque paintings in gold-gilded frames hung on the walls. At the center of the

47

marble floor—designed as a mosaic pattern in the shape of some kind of animal Oscar couldn't quite determine from the doorway—another video monitor was set up on a stand.

As each of them shuffled in behind him, Oscar and Henry looking over the massive foyer, Joy once again checking her phone for service, a man's voice echoed from somewhere deeper inside the house: "*Hello? Is anybody here?*"

THE HOURGLASS

Hello?" the man called out. "*Is anybody here?*"

Joy heard uncertainty in the voice, edging toward the same fear she'd felt upon reentering the house. She'd known this was a bad idea, that the last time she'd trusted her dead husband she'd been humiliated and humbled. She didn't really think he'd have left her there to die if she'd never solved his puzzle—he hadn't been quite that far gone then—but what she hadn't told the others was that he'd let her piss herself rather than open the door for her, that he'd grinned sheepishly at her embarrassment and said, "My poor baby," as if he'd come home to find she'd fallen down the stairs rather than locked her in a room himself with a single bottle of water for six fucking hours.

Henry's plea had gotten under her skin, that had been the first chip in her resolve. She didn't know if he was innocent or guilty, but she could tell that whatever he'd done in the past, he seemed to be gentle and intelligent and kind. He'd suffered in prison, that much was clear, some at the hands of the man in charge of him here. She didn't want him to suffer a "living Hell" simply because she was worried Alexei would embarrass or mildly harm them.

More than that, it was Alexei's final statement about his assets being liquidated and given to Infiniti Enterprises that ultimately changed her mind. Early in their marriage, long before they'd dissolved their joint accounts and gone their separate ways, she'd spotted several large donations to this so-called "foundation," whatever it happened to be. She'd questioned him about it but he'd been evasive as to what exactly the fund did with its donations. From then on, she hadn't seen any further transactions to the fund, but Alexei had grown more secretive and quicker to anger. All of this had culminated with her discovering Alexei and those strange men in the basement, digging a shaft into the floor of the room she'd escaped only a few months prior.

She'd looked up Infiniti Enterprises on the internet but hadn't found much useful information. It had several high-profile donors, including CEOs of Fortune 500 companies, billionaire hedge fund managers and financiers, many of whom were involved with the World Economic Forum and had upped their net worth by countless more billions since the fund was created. Whatever it *actually* did, it seemed like some kind of pyramid scheme and tax shelter for uber rich elites.

Alexei's comment was bait, she knew, meant to taunt and toy with her from beyond the grave. But she'd happily swallow hook, line and sinker if it meant Infiniti wouldn't get their hands on that money.

Anyone but them.

"*Hello?*" came the voice again.

"We're in here," Joy called back. She tucked the cell phone back in her pocket. "Still no service. This whole house is probably a giant—"

Before she could finish, the door to the small room they'd entered through clicked shut, sealing them inside.

The foyer smelled like Alexei's cologne—Krasnaya Moskova, the same brand his father had worn in the "Old Country," as the old man had called his and Alexei's native land of Siberia. It was mingled with stale cigar smoke, one of Alexei's favorite vices. Standing here ensconced in his miasma made Joy think fondly of him for the first time in years. The feeling didn't sit well with what she knew of him now.

Atkins dragged Henry over to the door to their left, which had opened on the drawing room when Joy was last here. Who knew what it was now, aside from locked, which of course she'd expected, even though Atkins hadn't. They tried the other doors next, which were also locked.

A moment later a tall man with small round spectacles, short-cropped silver hair and silver streaks in his black beard wandered out from below the right stairwell. He wore a tweed jacket, corduroy pants and a polka-dotted ascot ruffling out from his open dress shirt collar.

"Oh, thank God," the man said. "I don't know why on Earth I decided to continue after that first puzzle. I suppose one or more of the gods and goddesses of wealth must have lured me in with the promise of good fortune. Regardless, I'm glad to see your faces."

"How did you get in here?" Joy asked. "Which door?"

The man glanced back in curiosity. "Under the stairs here," he said, nodding toward the south staircase. "It locked behind me, if that's the reason you ask. Quite firmly, I should add."

Joy let out a depressed groan.

"You're on your own?" Oscar asked.

"I assumed we all were. The four of you arrived as an ensemble?"

They nodded.

"Well, I certainly didn't need the help. The next puzzles should be quite easy with more heads to rap together."

"What now?" Oscar said. "There should be six of us."

"Seven," Henry said, reminding them of the extra body in the room. Atkins clenched his jaw.

The newcomer noticed Henry and took a step back, as Oscar had earlier. "Is he... safe?"

"Long as I'm alive he is," Atkins grunted.

"Then I suppose we wait here for the other two," the newcomer said. He indicated the video monitor. "It looks like our host has another message to pass along. In the meantime, perhaps introductions are in order. I'm Dr. Rudyard Thomas, associate professor and director of the archeology graduate program at Olympia University. You may call me Rudy or Doctor but never Rudyard, thank you."

Joy introduced herself first, to which Rudy said, "Ah, yes, I thought you looked familiar, wonderful to meet you," shaking her hand vigorously. Oscar and Henry followed. Rudy shook Oscar's hand with the same vigor and simply nodded at Henry.

Atkins reluctantly grunted his surname.

"Yes, I see that on your lapel," Rudy said, pointing out the nametag. "Well, it's a pleasure to meet you all. I don't suppose any of you knew the deceased, either?"

"He was my ex-husband. The others didn't know him."

"I see. Was your husband—*ex*, beg pardon—was he a sadist, by any chance?"

Rudy pronounced sadist like the emotion, saddest, causing Joy to bark a laugh.

"I guess you could say that."

"I thought as much. One would rather have to be, I'd think, to devise such a devious form of bequeathment."

"That or a real prick," Atkins said.

Rudy chuckled at this, wiping his glasses on the breast of his jacket.

"Wait a minute, what happens if the other two don't solve their puzzle?" Oscar said. "Alexei said it had to be all of us. Or what if they choose to leave?"

"A pertinent question. One I suspect none of us are equipped to answer at the moment." Rudy goggled at one of the paintings. "Is that a Caravaggio?" He broke from the group to admire it more closely.

The others stood a moment in silence, looking over the large foyer. All but Joy, who'd admired the Caravaggio— *Nativity with St. Francis and St. Lawrence*, the only painting Alexei would store in the basement with his wines and cognacs when guests were invited, which Joy had later discovered was because it had been listed as stolen in Sicily in 1969—and the Rembrandt and all of the other originals Alexei had brought into their home over the years, and instead noticed the only thing other than the television that was out of place.

High above the room, on the wall of the second-floor landing, hung a digital clock counting down from one minute... fifty-five seconds... fifty seconds...

What happens when the counter reaches zero? she wondered.

"What kind of animal is that on the floor?" Henry asked.

Joy turned briefly from the clock to look at the mosaic in

the tiles. She shrugged. "It wasn't there when I lived here."

"That would be Cerberus," Rudy said, turning back from the tenebrist nativity scene. "The three-headed guard dog of the underworld. Faithful companion to Hades, Lord of the Dead."

40... 39...

"Some folks call it Hell, I call it Hades, mmhmm," Oscar muttered in a bad Southern accent.

Rudy smiled. "*Sling Blade*?"

"I like movies."

31... 30...

"Rather good fortune you're stuck here with a movie star then, isn't it?"

Oscar shrugged and nodded. "Could be worse."

22... 21...

"Hey, guys," Joy said. When they turned, she nodded toward the clock.

"What's with the timer?" Henry asked.

Rudy gave it a thoughtful look. "Whatever it is, I suspect we'll discover in a moment."

12... 11...

As the seconds counted down from ten, Joy became certain she didn't want to find out what would happen at zero, though she suspected it was just another of Alexei's games.

At five, the monitor hummed on, Alexei smiling from the darkness, his face lit like his precious Caravaggio.

The timer reached zero, and Alexei said, "Time's up," clucking his tongue against the roof of his mouth in the way that had always annoyed Joy, when she'd done something not to his satisfaction. "It appears one or more of our players failed to solve their puzzle in time. Sadly, they must be penalized."

And suddenly a large rectangular segment of the wall with the "lost" Caravaggio and Dürer and the arched doors to the dining hall began to slide away under the staircase, revealing what appeared to be a glass wall behind it.

Two women stood within a vestibule much like the one Joy and the others had entered through, except the walls appeared to be made of sandstone blocks, and the roof had a glassed opening, something like a skylight.

The women argued with each other, clearly raising their voices, despite being inaudible behind the glass, while looking around the room in frustration and picking up objects—a blue and gold snake carved from wood with a gold circle resting on its head, what looked like a set of skeleton keys, a polished brass hand mirror—then setting them down again. One of the women was dressed in all black, from her leather biker jacket to her skin-tight black jeans and boots—the kind of outfit Helen Arrowheart would wear riding her Lotus C-01 motorcycle. The other wore a polka-dotted dress and flat, black pumps with her hair in a retro pinup style under a scarf.

"Jessica?" Rudy said, stepping closer to the glass.

"Who?"

"Olympia's former Dean of Admissions. The woman in black. That's Jessica Danvers."

"She doesn't much look like a college admin," Joy said.

"She used to ride a motorcycle to work most days. We called that her 'Easy Rider' outfit. I suspect she rides it more often than not now she's retired. But what in blue blazes is she doing here?"

"What in *blue blazes* are any of us doing here?" Henry shot back.

Rudy ignored him, moving closer to the glass. "Perhaps we could help them. Those objects appear to be ancient Egyptian, particularly the hand mirror. The room I entered through was Babylonian, which was fortunate, seeing as my research interests lie mainly in the religious history of Mesopotamia."

"Ours was Japan," Oscar said.

Joy waved at the women and called "*Hello!*" but neither of them responded.

"It's a soundproof two-way mirror," Henry said. "They can't hear or see us."

"How do you know?" Oscar said.

"Because I used to be a detective," the prisoner replied. "Interrogation rooms use the same thing."

Oscar's mouth closed audibly. He approached the glass and knocked. Again, neither woman noticed. He pounded on it, rattling the glass in its frame. No response from the women inside. "I guess you're right. We can't help them."

"What do we do if they don't solve it? Stand here with our dicks in our hands?" Atkins said.

Joy turned to her dead husband, his face frozen in a grin on the screen.

What happens to them if they don't get out, you fucking maniac? she wanted to ask him. *What would you have done to us?*

"Ah!" Rudy exclaimed, drawing Joy's attention from the screen. "Do you see it? There's a small brass plate inside the door, marked with hieroglyphs representing the serpent deity, Apep or Apophis, the ancient Egyptian embodiment of chaos."

Joy looked past the arguing women to what appeared to be a door made of the same sandstone as the rest of the room. She thought it might allow passage through to a hallway that would eventually connect to this room, as Rudy's had.

"Apep was the enemy of Ra," he explained, "the sun god. Reflect the sun's rays from the roof opening onto the plate using the hand mirror with enough intensity, *et viola*, the door will open."

"I'm sticking with this guy," Atkins joked.

"We're *all* staying together," Joy said. "That's the only way we'll make it out of here alive."

Rudy raised an eyebrow at her. "A tad melodramatic, *n'est ce pas?*"

Joy returned his challenge with a glare. "I was married to that man for fifteen years. He *changed*. The last time I saw him… he was not the same man I married."

Rudy opened his mouth to challenge her, then closed it again, leaving the words unspoken.

"A lot less living, for one thing," Atkins quipped.

Joy ignored him. If the women weren't able to get out on their own, maybe she could find out where they'd be let out if they did solve the puzzle and open it from the other side.

She headed off in that direction. As she passed under the shadow of the right stairway, Oscar said, "Something's happening," with dread in his tone.

Joy turned and peered inside the glassed-in room made to look like the entrance to an Egyptian pyramid. At first, she didn't notice what Oscar had seen. Then the women inside looked up in surprise which quickly became horror. Sand was pouring in through the skylight. The glass no longer covered the opening.

Joy couldn't hear what the woman in the polka-dot dress—whom she thought of as Kay, after Sophia Loren's character who'd worn a similar dress in Sidney Lumet's *That Kind of Woman*—shouted at Jessica when she pointed toward the opening. But she could read the woman's lips, mainly because she'd thought the same thing.

We need to get up there.

Jessica rushed toward a stone altar about the size and height of the storage bench Joy had in her foyer. The tendons in her neck pulled taut as she tried to move it toward the skylight. Meanwhile, sand had already covered the floor, several inches deep. As she called to Kay, who then hurried to the other end of the altar, it looked like they were walking on an indoor beach.

"We have to do something," Oscar said, a look of fear on his reflection in the glass.

"What *can* we do?" Rudy asked. The man appeared to be studying the proceedings as if they were nothing more than insects in an ant farm, though he did appear to have an affinity for his Dean of Admissions, judging by the slight smile he'd worn when speaking of her motorcycle outfit.

Joy nodded, searching the foyer for something to heave against the glass. "He's right." She spotted two of Alexei's precious vases on either side of the kitchen door, standing on pedestals she remembered were heavy plaster. "Help me," she said to Oscar.

Together the women in the room tried to carry the altar toward the aperture, which had become the neck of an hourglass. Sand poured through it on all sides. A growing heap collected under the opening, and the objects in the room were coated in a thin layer. The women coughed and choked as the sand swirled around them. They dragged the altar across the floor—the sand appeared to make that easier, at least—and dropped it under the former skylight. Sand poured over their heads and shoulders, and they quickly stepped out of the way, shaking and brushing it off their bodies and hair.

Joy and Oscar hurried past the stairs. She noticed as they arrived at the kitchen door that Oscar was holding his lower back. "Are you gonna be okay with this?"

With a wince, he said, "I'll be fine."

"Okay." She tried the kitchen doors, just in case. They were locked, just as she'd expected. She removed the Qing Dynasty vase and plate and placed them on the floor to the side. "On the count of three, we lift."

Joy crouched and grabbed the base of the pedestal. Oscar gripped the top. "One… two… three," she said, and lifted from the bottom. Oscar caught the weight of the top and grunted. She probably should have asked Atkins or Henry, but it would have been a big production trying to get them both over here and with the amount of sand pouring through the opening, she didn't suspect they had much time. The archeologist didn't look like he could bench press a terrier, so she hadn't bothered to ask him.

The sand had completely buried the altar by the time Oscar and Joy returned with the pedestal. The women now stood in it up to their shins. Jessica brushed away the sand from the altar and climbed up. She waved for Kay to join her. As the other woman stepped up onto the altar, the sand had already filled the room up to her knees.

Joy and Oscar carried the pedestal bowlegged to the glass wall. "Three count again, Oscar. We're gonna use it like a ram," she said. "You sure you're good?"

He nodded, though his upper lip glistened with sweat.

"Okay." On "one" they swung the pedestal forward and back. Same with "two." On three they rammed it at the glass. It slipped out of Oscar's grip and struck at an angle with a loud *BOOM*. Still, it should have at least cracked the glass. Instead, it left a chunk of plaster dust and a purple liquidlike smear and fell to the floor, splitting in half on the marble tiles.

"I'm sorry," he said.

Joy swallowed her disappointment. "It's okay."

"It's a screen," Henry said.

"Beg pardon?"

"They can't hear us or see us because they aren't behind a glass wall. That's a giant TV screen."

"That makes no sense," Joy said.

"That purple stain," Henry said, pointing at the spot where the pedestal connected with the glass. "That's LCD fluid."

Atkins narrowed his eyes. "He's right. That happened to my phone when I dropped it on the floor of the john."

"There's an image," Rudy muttered.

"That means there's nothing we can do," Oscar said, his tone grave as he'd apparently reached the same conclusion Joy had earlier. Those women could die in there and there wasn't a damn thing the five of them could do to stop it.

It was exactly what Alexei would have wanted. To make them watch. To make them participants in someone else's demise.

It was all a game to him. Life. Death. Everything. Just an elaborate game played on a cosmic chess board. Or an escape room.

Joy watched as both women leapt into the air, reaching for the opening. Even standing on the pedestal, stretching their arms as high as they could, they fell short by at least three feet. The sand poured over their heads and shoulders, as deep now as the altar was tall. They slipped in the sand and fell, only to climb back up to try again.

Jessica and Kay looked at each other in despair. There was no way out. They would die buried in sand.

"I can't look at this any longer," Rudy said with a sour expression. He trudged away and sat on the foot of the stairs, head in his hands.

"There must be something we can do," Oscar said with a hopeless look toward Joy, as if she had all the answers.

She shook her head. "They could be anywhere... they might not even be in the house."

"It might've already happened," Henry said. "They could've shot this earlier."

"Why the hell would they do that?" Atkins barked.

"I don't know. Or maybe it's a trick. Maybe all of this is an elaborate prank. They could be—" He turned his gaze on Joy. "—they could be actors, for all we know."

Joy shook her head. "This isn't a game. He might want us to think that, but those women are in danger. We're *all* in danger, if we don't solve every one of his puzzles." She pointed at the giant screen. "This is gonna keep happening again and again, until there's only one of us left standing."

"Two," Atkins said. When everyone but Rudy turned to him, he added, "I'm not supposed to be here, remember?"

"Someone is watching this other than us," Oscar said. "They wouldn't just let those people die."

"You don't know Alexei like I do."

Again, Oscar closed his mouth audibly.

With sand up to their shoulders, every object in the room smothered, the women appeared hopeless, out of options. They tried to climb to the top but the rush of sand from the opening pummeled them, the surface too yielding. They were covered from head to toe. They choked, spitting out beige clouds.

Then came the snakes.

Joy gasped as they tumbled through the opening, one after the other, the first landing in the sand between the women in the room and slithering quickly away, another dropping on Jessica's head, which she batted away in terror, the third behind Kay, who twisted to watch it. Each snake was as thick and black as a bicycle tire with scales and flat flanges surrounding their heads.

"Oh, God," Henry muttered.

"What *are* those?" Oscar asked.

"Egyptian cobras," Rudy said. He'd gotten up from the stairs when Joy reacted to the snakes, and returned to the group. "The deity Apep is often called the Serpent from the Nile, though cobras were typically associated with Wadjet, a goddess of cultists in Lower Egypt. I should have known from the cobra *uraei* among the objects."

59

While Rudy spoke the first snake wound its way into the far corner of the room. The one Jessica batted away stood and hissed at her. She tried to back away from it but the sand was too high to push through. All she could do was stand there, immobile, watching it in absolute terror.

Fear slithered up Joy's spine as she watched them. "Cobras are poisonous, aren't they?"

"*Venomous*," Oscar said. "Poison is ingested. Venom is injected."

The third snake rose up, hissing at Kay. Her eyes went wide, then her fear became determination. In the next moment she snatched out and grabbed the snake just under its head. Then she turned to face her companion and thrust the snake toward her.

"No," Joy gasped.

"Dear God," Rudy muttered.

The cobra's fangs came out and pierced Jessica's throat. While she jerked, her eyes and mouth wide in terror and agony, the other snake darted at her, biting her right hand. Kay threw her living weapon into the corner of the room. Jessica batted the second snake away and grabbed Kay by the throat, blood spilling from the puncture marks in her own. Kay punched her square in the nose. Jessica fell back and Kay climbed up onto her, pulling herself out of the sand using Jessica's shoulders.

Oscar's hands tented below his nose, as if in prayer.

Rudy shook his head despondently. "How could she… how could she *do* that?"

"You'd be surprised what people will do to stay alive," Henry said. Then he shrugged. "Or not."

Jessica struggled and convulsed while Kay climbed on top of her, but with the venom coursing through her veins she was already losing the battle. She grasped at Kay's ankles as Kay rose to a crouch, her feet planted on Jessica's stomach and shoulder, wobbling like she was trying to stand on a surfboard. From there she reached up, spitting and shaking away the still pouring sand, and grabbed the edge of the opening. As she pushed herself up and through, Jessica sank below the surface, her final anguished cry filling her mouth with sand.

Then both women were gone, Kay escaped through the opening in the roof, Jessica buried beneath the sand.

The wall screen went black.

"Jesus Christ," Atkins grunted. "Did that actually just happen?"

"How could she do that?" Rudy repeated flatly, moving away from the glass.

"Oh, goodness," Alexei said from the small screen, as if in reply. "If only they could have worked in solidarity to solve the puzzle, perhaps they could both join you now. Unfortunately, that wasn't the case."

"You fucking monsters!" Joy shouted up at the ceiling, hoping whoever was watching could hear her. "You didn't have to kill her!"

"Kinda makes you wonder what he had in store for *us*," Atkins said with a bitter chuckle, to which Henry nodded gravely.

"I told you," Joy said, shaking her head. "I told you this was a bad idea."

Atkins turned his scowl on her. "Then why did you say yes?"

She considered telling them, if only to relieve her guilt. But she said, "I have my reasons," and left it at that.

"Exactly," Henry said. "We all have our reasons. And none of us knew him but you."

"So it's my fault?"

The others looked toward Henry. "I'm not saying that. I... look, we're all here now. We know what this is all about. This isn't jungle law. None of us are gonna murder each other to survive. For all we know, those snakes were devenomed—"

"Venomoids," Oscar said.

"Whatever. You said it yourself, your husband—"

Joy didn't even bother correcting him this time.

"—he was some kind of sadist. He locked you in a room for six hours with a compass and a bottle of water. That's a man who likes to play games, who likes to toy with people, even the people closest to him. Who knows if this wasn't some kind of Stanford Prison Experiment, and those two failed the test? If

61

they worked together, like he said—" Henry nodded toward the monitor, "—maybe they both would've made it out alive."

Joy wasn't sure she believed it, but she had to admit he made a good case. Still, only one of them had a gun, and another could quite possibly be a murderer. Two, if you counted Kay, the woman in the polka-dot dress.

As if summoned by Joy's thoughts, a husky female voice called down from the second-floor landing: "Well, hey there, party people! Who's ready for some escape room fun?"

THE BOOK

"YOU KILLED HER!" Joy shouted up at the new woman.

The gang's all here, Henry thought.

From where he stood, he could see right up her polka-dot dress, her tanned bare legs leading up to a pair of black boy shorts. She had sand in her poufed auburn hair and sticking to her freckled face from sweat. Henry hadn't seen a woman's bare legs in almost two years, let alone their underwear, and his eyes lingered longer than he'd intended. He turned his gaze upward in time to see the woman's smile falter at Joy's accusation.

"You were *watching* us? And what, you just stood there while the two of us *almost died*?"

"One of you *did* die," Joy snapped back.

The new woman headed for the stairs, heels clacking on the hardwood floor. "Yeah, well *both* of us would've died if I hadn't done something. You think I wanted to…" Her face contorted with guilt, an expression Henry was all too familiar with, before returning to a look of indignation. "…to *do* that? You think I would've done that if they'd given me any other choice?"

Joy crossed to the bottom of the stairs as the woman descended. "The snakes could have been venomless."

"Venomoids," Oscar said again. Joy shot him a death stare over her shoulder.

"Let me ask you something," the woman said, pausing in the middle of the stairway with one manicured hand on the railing. "You were married to the guy. Do *you* believe that?"

Joy opened her mouth to speak. She closed it again and said nothing.

"Yeah, I know you, Joy Reese. And I looked the rest of you people up, too. Henry Hall, currently serving a fifteen-year sentence on a plea bargain for premeditated murder. Dr. Rudolph Thomas, professor of archeology at Olympia University. I'm guessing that's the beanpole," she said, pointing to the man. "We sure could've used your help in there, so thanks for nothing. And Dr. Oscar Evans, head virologist at Freedom Health Hospital. Would've been nice to know that about the snakes, just by the way."

"What was the name of the woman you murdered?" Joy snapped.

The other woman sputtered with a shake of her head. "Is it murder when animals kill each other in the wild? Law of the jungle, sister. Kill or be killed."

Henry spoke before Joy could parry back. "You seem to know all of us. What's your name?"

The woman flashed a smile. "You're better looking than your mugshots, you know that? I'm Ileana." She gave Joy a direct look as she added, "Thanks for asking."

"What's your *last* name?" Atkins asked, though Henry was relatively sure Atkins knew her as well as he did himself. How could they not, considering who she was?

"My last name is none of your business," she said. "The woman they stuck me with was Jessica Danvers, though. She was the dean at Rudy's university, weirdly enough, until she got caught up in that nepo baby scandal a few years back. So don't feel too bad about her. She wasn't exactly a good person."

Joy all but screamed, "*Does that mean she deserved to die?*"

"No! Of course not. What, do you think *I* did? You think *any* of us do?"

"Good people often get caught up in circumstances beyond their control," Rudy lectured, adjusting his cravat. "One could look no further than what you were just party to—unless, of course, you don't consider yourself a good person?"

"What do you do?" Oscar asked, hands clasped together

below his waist, looking desperate to alleviate the tension.

"She's a California state senator," Atkins said, gritting his teeth with a hand resting on his baton as if he was inches away from beating her to within an inch of her life. "Ileana Athanasiou."

"That's right," Ileana said. "Democratic Representative for District 41, Avalon County."

"She voted *for* Prop. 57 and *against* bail requirements for violent offenders," Atkins told the others. "Thanks for making my job a lot harder, Senator."

"Bail requirements are unconstitutional," she shouted at him, as if across the party aisle. "The Eighth Amendment *clearly* states—"

"*Are you all quite done?*"

All eyes returned to the television at the sound of the dead man's voice. The man himself smiled faintly, then continued. "You are gathered here today to participate in the Last Will and Testament of Alexei Fyodor Vasiliev: my magnum opus, the last of my many puzzles. As you've seen, these rooms can be quite deadly. Those who survive will be awarded not just my entire estate, including the house in which you stand, but *anything your heart desires*. I will give you the world."

Henry noticed Joy flinch at the words, as if she'd been slapped.

"Those who do not..." Alexei shrugged slightly. "I am sorry but there will be more casualties."

"This is illegal," Ileana said.

Atkins snorted. "No shit, sister."

"However," the dead man continued, "this *is* a game. It can be bested by using your intellects, your wits, and by working together. If you are at odds with each other, it isn't unlikely that none of you will survive the game. But if you *do* survive, know that you have bested me, Alexei Vasiliev, the world's foremost puzzle master. Good luck to you all."

The television screen went black.

"Well, that's great," Ileana said. "Anyone else here feel comforted by that?" She did jazz hands as she announced sarcastically: "The Great Alexei Vaseline, world's foremost puzzle maker!"

"Master," Henry said. "He said puzzle *master*. It feels like that's an important distinction, at least to him."

"I'm not calling him that."

Henry turned to Joy, who merely shook her head.

"Question," Oscar said, raising a hand. "He's dead... so how did he know that woman—"

"Ms. Danvers," Rudy reminded him.

Oscar paused briefly, clearly rattled by the interjection. "How did he know she died in there?" he finished.

Henry regarded the wall screen a moment, with its chalk-dust blemish and purple smear where Oscar and Joy had tried to crack it, then turned back to face the blank TV screen. The others followed his gaze. No one spoke for several moments.

"Is it possible..." Rudy began, stroking his beard as he looked at Joy. "...could your husband—*ex*-husband, beg pardon—is it possible he's not really dead?"

Again, Joy opened her mouth to speak and said nothing. She looked at the television screen, then frowned. "I don't know what to think," she said finally.

"He could be dead still," Oscar suggested. "They could've filmed a bunch of different variations. Like that interactive movie on Netflix."

"*Bandersnatch*," Rudy replied. "I rather enjoyed that, though I don't often watch television."

"Right. So maybe he's got a version for each of us, or at least for each puzzle. He doesn't *have* to know who died when or if we all survive. They just have to play the right clip at the right time."

"They?" Ileana said. "They who?"

Oscar pointed toward the high ceiling. "The eye in the sky."

"People are *watching* us?" She seemed shocked, as if she'd never considered it. "*Recording* this?"

"That's how we saw what you did," Joy said. "That used to be a giant screen."

"Shit." Ileana balled her hands into fists and started pacing the floor, heels alternately clacking on hardwood and thudding over the Persian rug. "Shit, shit, shit..." *Thud, thud, clack,*

clack…

"What's her deal?" Atkins grunted.

"Probably wondering how she'll spin it if she makes it out of here," Joy said.

"Hey." Henry reached out as Ileana passed him again and grabbed her by the shoulder. She snapped out of it and looked down at his hand, her lips curling into a sneer. He removed it quickly.

"A compliment is not an invitation," she said.

"I'm just—" He licked his lips, his mouth suddenly parched. "We have to be present, if we're gonna beat this thing. Not thinking about what might happen if we actually survive."

She eyed him a moment longer, then softened. "You're right. He's right," she said to the others. "We have to focus. We have to work together. What happened in that room…" Her lower lip trembled. "I am so… sorry. That wasn't me. Something took over me and I just… I did what I thought I had to do to survive. Any one of you would do the same."

"We're not *murderers*."

"Joy," Henry said.

She looked at him and seemed to take his meaning, but couldn't help herself. "No, Henry. I can tell acting when I see it. She doesn't give a shit about what she did. She only wants us to *think* she does. She's already trying to *twist* this into something that'll benefit her next campaign."

"You know what? Fuck you, Joy Reese." Ileana crossed the room while jabbing a finger at her accuser. "I see right through you, too. Don't think I don't know an opportunist when I smell one."

"All right, just calm down, ladies," Atkins said.

"*Excuse me?* I am calm!"

Atkins rolled his eyes. "Yeah. Calm as clams."

"I'm not turning my back on this woman for a second," Joy said. "And I suggest the rest of you not trust her, either."

"Fine. Don't trust me. You can all fucking die in here for all I care."

Silence fell over the occupants of the foyer as they all cooled down and looked over the room.

"Wait a second," Oscar said, looking at the TV stand. He opened the cabinet, behind which was a large pro-tape player with dozens of buttons and knobs and VU meters, like the kind they used to have at the station. "There's a machine here. It looks like an old Betamax player."

"U-Matic," Rudy said. "Olympia used to have them in the film department."

"Why would they have that?" Joy asked, joining them. "Something this old can't play HD video."

"She's right," Oscar said. "Unless it was letterboxed 4:3 he wouldn't have filled the screen like that."

While they worked it out, Henry had remained outside the huddle with Atkins. "Press eject," he suggested.

Oscar reached for the button... then hesitated and withdrew his finger. He looked back at the others with suspicion. "What if it's a trap?"

Atkins grunted. "We can't act like everything's a trap in here, otherwise we won't do anything."

"Hang on," Ileana said, opening her purse, which Henry only just now noticed she'd managed to hold onto despite being a hair's width from death. She took out a tube of lipstick and held it toward the machine. "Which one is it?"

"This one here," Oscar said, pointing at a blue button in the bottom row.

Ileana used the lipstick to press it. The machine made a high whine as the gears wound, then the tape ejected from its mouth. Only it wasn't a tape. It was a scuffed brown leather object the same shape as the opening.

"Is that...?" Joy began.

"A book," Oscar said, taking it out of the machine. He opened it and flipped through the pages of thick parchment with rough edges. "It's empty. All the pages are blank."

As he said it, the two pages began to fill with inked art and intricate symbols, like a Polaroid photograph developing before their eyes. They were far more complicated than anything Henry had ever painted or sketched himself, though they appeared to have been etched onto the pages in a fever dream, anatomical studies of interdimensional beings.

"*Oh my God*," Ileana breathed.

"Must be invisible ink," Joy said, looking back at the others. "Alexei loved that trick, ever since he was little. He used to write messages to his..." She trailed off, before finishing, "...little brother."

"Lemon juice, reacting to heat," Henry said. "I used to have that in my detective kit when I was a kid."

Rudy looked up from the book with concern. "Those images, that language... it's cuneiform." The others looked at him for explanation. "Akkadian, I believe. Pre-Sumerian in any case."

"Can you read it?"

Rudy shook his head. "It's not my area of expertise, I'm afraid. If my damned cell worked, I could ring a colleague. Jason might know. Or Li Wei."

"What are those... *things*?" Oscar asked, nodding at the images. His Adam's apple clicked audibly as he swallowed.

"That seated figure looks quite similar to the depiction of Apep found in the Coffin Texts of Ancient Egypt, later copied into the Book of the Dead."

"*The Necronomicon?*" Oscar asked, clearly unsettled.

Rudy shook his head patronizingly. "The stuff of pure fiction, I'm afraid. The true Book of the Dead, the *Egyptian* Book of the Dead, while technically the first known *literal* grimoire, is merely a series of magic spells meant to assist the dead in his travels throughout the *Duat*, the Egyptian underworld. This is the same region the sun god Ra was believed to have traveled during the night. That's him standing beside our friend with the snake on his face," he added, pointing to a falcon-headed man with a staff in one hand and a sphere perched on his head. In his other hand he held an *ankh*, which Henry knew from a childhood obsessed with the eerie and macabre was a symbol of eternal life.

"What's this?" Joy asked, pointing to the image at the top of the second page of a burning sun being swallowed by a similarly shaped but hideous-looking dark blob with curled snakes in the place of rays. It was surrounded by more of Rudy's cuneiform lettering.

"That, I suppose, is meant to be the true form of Apep. It looks something like an eclipse, *n'est ce pas*? Imagine yourself an ancient Egyptian peering into the sky in horror as your god is swallowed by his rival... what you might have believed."

"The end of the world," Henry said. The others turned to him. He shrugged.

"Perhaps. Though the fear would have only lasted a few moments. At the end of an eclipse, Ra always triumphs, carrying the sun with him."

Huddled closely over the book with Oscar and Rudy, Joy looked up at him with genuine fear in her eyes. "What if Ra didn't win?"

Rudy reared back to stand. He thought about it for a moment before replying. "Then, I suppose, that *would* be the end of the world. Wouldn't it?"

"Well, okay," Ileana said. "This is fun and all, but we've still got some more puzzles to solve. We all still want to get out of here, right? We should probably get moving."

"She's right," Atkins said. "We can't stand here looking at picture books all day."

"True enough," Rudy agreed, though his cautious gaze lingered on the book, the lenses of his glasses magnifying his eyes to comically large proportions. "Though I suspect this book may bear more importance on our predicament than we might think."

"How so?" Henry asked. He'd had a similar feeling and been unable to ascribe a reason to it.

"Well, suppose for a moment this *is* just lemon juice on a page. How then did the exact images corresponding to the loss we saw in that room—" He pointed toward the wall screen. "—show up on these pages? Why not any of the other deities?"

Joy frowned. "What do you mean?"

"It could have been the three of you who ran out of time," Rudy said.

Joy's brow furrowed at this.

"Or you," Atkins grunted.

"Yes, or me. Though much more unlikely, given my expertise. What I mean to say is, yes, *perhaps* the relative temperature of the room caused the invisible ink or lemon juice to appear as if by magic, *but...* and this is a very *important* but... how likely is it that the outcome of Ms. Danvers and Miss—"

"Missus," Ileana said.

He smiled patiently. "Mrs. Athanasiou, thank you—how likely is it that whoever placed this book here for us to discover was able to predict that Apep would conquer Ra? Why not your Japanese demon, whatever that might have been? Or my Pazuzu, from Babylonia?"

The others shared a mystified look, then returned their attention to the images in the book. Oscar closed it quickly with a clap and held it out. "Someone take this," he said. "I think I'm going to be sick."

Joy took the book from him, holding it at arm's length, the way Ileana had held the snake, while Oscar rushed toward a standing vase in the corner of the room. His retching echoed hollowly within the ceramic, thick liquid splashing into it. From where Henry stood, it looked to be a priceless puke bucket.

"You're saying..." Atkins barked a laugh. "...you're saying this book *is* magic. For-real magic."

"I'm not *saying* anything concrete. I merely suggest we keep it with us, and not take it lightly."

Henry nodded. "I agree. However it works, it obviously means something. I'll take it, Joy." The shackles jingled as he held out his hands to her.

She gave him a relieved look as she handed the book to him.

The first thing Henry noticed was it was much lighter than he expected. The leather cover was light colored and smoothly textured, possibly goat or lambskin. Running his right hand over it caused him to vividly recall his day on the witness stand at his own trial, one hand on the Bible while swearing to tell the whole truth and nothing but the truth. He'd seen dozens of criminals—from murderers to thieves to child rapists—perform the same gesture and had never imagined he'd have to do it on his own behalf. It was a surreal experience. All of it: the arrest, trial and aftermath. A whirlwind of lawyers' and journalists' questions. Sitting behind the defendant's table with his own lawyer, his union rep seated in the benches directly behind him as he pictured himself from a juror's point of view. Though when he thought of his day on the stand, he'd always remember the face of his little girl as Jeb Anderson lifted the sheet in the coroner's office. Picturing her always led to his last moments with her killer, the look of terror as Henry put the barrel of his gun to the man's head and squeezed the trigger.

What about this strange book reminded him of all of that?

Whatever it was, how and why the images appeared in it couldn't have been magic, not really. There had to be a rational explanation. Maybe there were other books inside the tape machine. Or maybe while the gears whirred and whined like an old tape machine ejecting a cassette, it had printed the image onto it.

Sure, that had to be it. There wasn't any reason to *fear* the Book, at the very least. Though for some reason he did decide it should be treated with a great deal of respect. Not *revered*, but respected. For that reason, he decided it should be thought of with a capital B, like the Bible.

It never occurred to him it could be an actual religious text, from a faith whose roots were older and deeper than any that came after it, though for some reason he unconsciously hugged the Book to his chest.

THE GAME

L et's get moving," Ileana said.

"Yeah," Oscar agreed with a pained wince. He was still holding his side, pressed against the pain in his bladder. Joy seemed to be deeply concerned for his well-being, but the others were too wrapped up in what was happening around them to notice, which was just fine by him. He didn't want to be a burden. He wanted to be a valuable part of the team. If they thought he needed to be babied, they wouldn't rely on him for anything. They'd let him sit it out on the sidelines, like his teachers had in gym class, because he'd been too nervous and fragile to play sports and had asked his parents, who'd also been doctors, to get one of their colleagues to sign a note exempting him from strenuous physical activity because of asthma he didn't have.

In retrospect it had been a bad idea all around. His parents should have pushed him to push himself. It wasn't like the benefits of physical activity were unknown in the 1980s, especially in the medical community. To be fair, Oscar had played with the few friends he'd had after school, riding bikes and horsing around. But he felt like he'd done himself a disservice by skipping out on gym class just because he didn't want to get hurt and worried he'd be last to be picked.

Was it ironic that he expected to spend the last days of his life in agony, after decades spent sheltering himself from any sort of pain, both physical and emotional?

"Which door did you come from?" he asked Ileana, hoping to prove himself useful immediately.

"Second floor on the right," she said, pointing up.

"So, it's probably not that way. Rudy, you said you came from under the right stairs, right?"

"Correct. There were two other doors to the left of it."

"Same as when I lived here," Joy added. "The kitchen and study."

"So, we've got five doors to choose from. How do we decide?"

"Maybe he gave us a clue," Henry suggested.

"Or perhaps the book contains one?" Rudy said, eyeing it cautiously.

Henry opened the book. The first two pages were the same with their illustrations of Ra and Apep and the strange cuneiform writing. Beyond that, the book appeared empty. "Nothing aside from what we already saw."

Ileana turned to the TV. "What was that he said at the end? 'I will give you the world.'"

"That wasn't a clue," Joy replied with a far-off look.

"How do you know?"

"Because he used to say that to me. It wasn't a clue, it was a dig at me. One last twist of the knife from beyond the grave."

"I'd wager it's not the last," Rudy said, "considering our current predicament."

"So… maybe we're supposed to pick a door," Oscar said, trying to pull them back on track.

"We checked them all," Atkins reminded him. "They're locked, remember?"

"That was before the last puzzle was… well," he said, clasping his hands below the waist. "Maybe they're open now."

The others looked at him.

"You said yourself, we can't stand around with our… you know… in our hands."

Ileana grinned at him, causing him to blush. He'd never been comfortable with sexual things. Even in med school he'd blushed while discussing the reproductive system. Intercourse itself had never interested him. What turned him on was the microscopic universe: microbial toxins, viruses, bacteria, fungi and dinoflagellates. He'd had one or two relationships in college but they'd fizzled out quickly when he'd suggested they take things a little more slowly before reaching the heavy petting stage. Single-celled organisms he could understand. Humans were tricky, apt to change their minds quickly and act out of character.

"All right," Henry agreed, their de facto leader. "Let's try the doors again."

While the others went off in groups of two, Henry with Atkins to the far end of the hall, Rudy with Ileana up the stairs, Joy followed Oscar toward the door straight ahead of them, directly across from the wall screen.

"This used to be where we'd host our singalongs," she said without emotion. "The grand ballroom. Alexei was a wonderful pianist."

The word made Oscar's blush deepen. They paused in front of the door. "You loved him once," he said. "Didn't you?"

She shrugged, then nodded. "I did, once upon a time. Or thought I did. 'I will give you the world,' he told me. For a few years, I actually believed it."

"You *have* the world," Oscar reminded her. "You're one of the highest paid actresses in Hollywood. Maybe he didn't give you that personally, but the two of you together... you made each other what you are. Or were. I don't know about his business, but I assume your connections became his connections and vice versa."

She considered it a moment, then said, "That's true. We wouldn't be where we are without each other." She looked back at the TV and frowned. "But where he is now is dead, and where I am is here, because of what *he* became. Or what *they* made him."

"What *who* made him?"

Joy shook her head. "Nothing. Never mind. Let's just try the door."

They both reached out and hesitated with their hands just about touching each other's, and the doorknob.

Oscar took his hand off his back and pulled his sleeve up over it. "I'll do it," he said, hoping having made the statement would give him the courage to follow through.

75

She smiled at him. The blush deepened.

Oscar grasped the door handle, expecting a shock or heat or extreme cold, even with his hand partly insulated, but he felt nothing. The handle jiggled but wouldn't turn. He tried pulling on it, but the door wouldn't budge.

"No joy," he said, then faced her with a sheepish grin. "So to speak."

She smiled back. "Hopefully the others have better luck."

They returned to the center of the room, next to the TV. Already Ileana and Rudy were descending the stairs. "All locked up there," Ileana said.

"Back here!" Henry called from the shadows beneath the second-floor landing.

"The kitchen?" Joy said.

Oscar didn't know if she was asking him or herself, but he followed her as she led the way to the swinging doors under the left stairwell.

Ileana and Rudy met them at the kitchen. There were porthole windows in each door, like in a restaurant, though the glass was smoky and opaque. Henry held the door on the right open a crack. Oscar could see only glimpses beyond the doors, but what he did see made his heart race.

"That was locked before," Rudy said.

Atkins sneered over his shoulder. "They all were."

"Should we go through?" Henry asked Joy.

Joy considered it a moment, then nodded stiffly. "I don't see what other choice we have."

"She's right," Ileana said. "Let's just get this over with."

Henry pulled the door the rest of the way open. Beyond was a morgue, complete with steel tables and corpses—or what *appeared* to be corpses—laid out under white sheets. There were four parallel tables, with a fifth perpendicular at the foot of them. The furthest of the four parallel tables lay empty aside from a sheet folded at the head. As Oscar looked over the room, he realized this was the perfect puzzle for his specialties, just like Rudy in the Babylonian room.

This puzzle was made for me, he thought.

From the winces and gasps of the others, they didn't share

76

the sentiment.

Dead bodies had never bothered Oscar. He'd been at his abuelo's bedside when he was six or seven as the wonderful old man passed away, had witnessed the weight lifted from his loved one's body, the final exhale leaving his lungs. Later in life, he'd spent countless hours examining them in med school with countless more autopsies performed in labs and makeshift morgues across the world. He'd been flown to Mexico City to handle the H1N1 outbreak in 2009, to Guinea during the Ebola epidemic in 2013, and to New York City in 2020, to work in the Covid-19 morgues, among several others.

"Those can't be real," Ileana said. "*Are they?*"

"Only one way to find out," Atkins said, jerking Henry into the room.

Joy followed them. Oscar took up behind her, holding the door behind him. Rudy and Ileana came last, seemingly reluctant.

Much of the equipment Oscar had in his own lab at the hospital was set up here: a state-of-the-art grossing station with stainless steel basin, polyethylene cutting boards and up-to-date computer pathology technology, a microtome for cutting accurate sections of tissue, an isolated tissue bath, a cytometer, an electron microscope. There was also a surgical tray containing various smaller instruments: a scalpel, a hypodermic syringe, surgical scissors, needle and thread, cotton balls and a bottle of iodine. Oscar had to fight the urge to rush right over and play with it all.

On the far wall three X-ray view boxes were set up above a worktable. Two displayed X-rays of a human midsection and head respectively. The third was empty, plain white. Below this was a digital balance scale. Above them, the words *MEDICE, CURA TE IPSUM*—Latin for the Biblical quote from Jesus meaning, "Physician, heal thyself"—were stuck to the wall in the same sort of flowery script as those hokey Live, Laugh, Love signs flaky people had in their living rooms.

Henry lifted up one of the sheets. Beneath was a young Asian woman with dark hair, gray skin and a neat little hole in her forehead the size of a bullet wound. "They're real," he said.

He placed the book on her chest and lifted her arm by the wrist. "No pulse. She's cold. Had to have been dead for a while."

"These are all..." Ileana swallowed audibly. "...*dead people?*"

No one else dared lift a sheet, but it was clear from their shapes that more bodies lay beneath them.

Henry picked up the book and pulled the sheet back up to cover the woman's face. Then he moved to the other end of the table to inspect the tag on the big toe of her right foot.

"Mary Chan," he read. "Date of death..." He scowled. "What day is today?"

"The eleventh," Joy said.

"Date of death, yesterday," Henry went on. "Cause of death: self-trepanation."

Ileana took a single step closer and examined the peaks and valleys of the sheeted body. "What's trepanation?"

"It means she bore a hole in her own skull," Rudy said.

Oscar added, "Like in that movie, *Pi*."

"The one with the tiger?" Ileana asked.

"That's *Life of Pi*. Pi like the number. Aronofsky's first film." Off Ileana's perplexed look, he said, "*Black Swan* guy? *Requiem for a Dream*?"

"I don't watch a lot of Oscar bait. No offense."

Oscar shrugged.

While he and Ileana discussed film, Henry and Atkins made the rounds, Henry lifting the sheets and checking the toe tags. The second was a middle-aged white man with his chest cracked open. Oscar startled at the sight of the dead man's face. He *knew* this man. In fact, he'd just spoken with him as late as last Thursday. He covered up the shock of recognition as best he could, but he feared Joy might have noticed. She'd been watching him like a hawk ever since he vomited in that vase in the foyer.

"Cause of death: internal hemorrhage," Henry read off the tag. Under the next sheet was a young black woman with her throat slit from ear to ear. Henry read the tag, "Cause of death: exsanguination and hypovolemic shock." Next was a Middle Eastern man in his mid- to late-fifties with a deep gash in his abdomen, similar to the wound the Apostle Thomas had to stick his finger into to believe Jesus had been resurrected. "Cause of death: septic shock." Henry lowered the sheet. "All of these people died within the last few days."

"What the fuck?" Ileana said, shaking her head in disbelief. "What the actual fuck?"

Henry lifted the final sheet and lowered it quickly with a wince. Atkins's eyes bugged out. Ileana yelped.

"What?" Joy said, standing near Oscar at the foot of the table. "Who is it?"

Oscar read the lower half of the tag on the woman's toe, the upper half hidden between her toes, the black lacquer on her toenails chipped from wear and time. The cause of death said, "PARALYSIS OF HEART AND LUNGS DUE TO SNAKE BITE."

"It's Jessica Danvers," Ileana said, shaking her head. "The woman I—" She stopped there, unable to go on, turning quickly and stalking away from the tables.

"The woman you murdered," Joy finished for her.

Atkins sputtered a laugh in Oscar's direction. "Guess they weren't venomoids, huh, pal?"

Oscar didn't reply. He *couldn't*. He'd turned away at the sound of the woman's name and now his attention was on the grossing station monitor, where something he couldn't possibly be seeing stared him straight in the face.

It was a photocopy of a statement from one of his first major jobs, signed at the bottom with his own name, in his own signature.

Oscar and his team hadn't been able to figure out what was wrong with the people in the Long Beach apartment complex. They'd exhibited a myriad of similar symptoms, ranging from ventricular arrythmia to subconjunctival hemorrhage, bleeding from the eyes. Along with standard symptoms like vomiting and diarrhea, it was presumed the tenants had contracted some kind of viral infection, though try as they might, Oscar's team had been unable to identify the culprit. They'd quarantined the subjects and given them generic antivirals, antibiotics and antifungals, but none of it seemed to work. In fact, their symptoms had only gotten worse. When the first of them passed away, he knew he'd have to move on to extreme measures, but he had no idea what to do.

With miraculously good timing, a representative from Apollo Pharmaceuticals came to him with a new drug, not yet approved to move on to the clinical trial stage, claiming they'd heard about the outbreak from one of Oscar's colleagues who later revealed he'd never spoken a word to anyone about it. They'd had success with irradicating a newly discovered virus in mice, with little to no adverse reactions. They claimed it was found in mouse droppings which could be accidentally ingested through various means. The superintendent had told Oscar and his team the building had a rodent problem—what he'd actually said was "mice the size of my fist," which was quite large and dirty—so Oscar looked over their research and agreed that, since no other treatment seemed to be helping these people, it would be prudent to at least try them on the drug.

Within a few days, the symptoms all cleared up. Their heart rates returned to normal. Their eyes healed. Their gastroenterological issues eased. They were cleared to go home, and Oscar and his team congratulated themselves on a job well done.

In retrospect, Oscar should've known something was suspicious about Apollo coming to him with the specific drug he'd needed at exactly the right time. When he was a boy, Oscar's priest had regaled his flock with a sermon in which he'd said the Devil was able to perform counterfeit miracles. He'd told them in times of need it might be difficult to tell the difference between fraud and the genuine article. That it would only be clear upon reflection. God, he'd said, would demand nothing in return but to walk with Him, whereas Satan would demand *everything*.

Of course, Oscar no longer believed in God. Not like he had back then. And in the moment, he'd just been grateful to be able to solve the mess swiftly before any of the other twenty-six patients died.

Upon reflection, it had become clear they'd infected these people deliberately, hoping to use them as a small test group to skirt clinical trials. The virus wasn't airborne, so it posed minimal danger to the general public compared to something that was. Like a non-polio enterovirus, it could only be contracted through close contact, drinking water, touching feces, eye, nose and mouth secretions or blister fluid. The likelihood that these people would have spread it outside of the building was even lower, due to the gastro symptoms coming on quickly and violently.

No one who contracted the virus would have wanted to be anywhere far from a toilet.

When Oscar confronted the Apollo representative, the man had told him they'd retained copies of the statements and data he'd faked, passing the outbreak off as a strain of enterovirus. He'd called their bluff, had told them to go to the Board. He would come clean himself if he had to. The rep had left with a clever quip Oscar couldn't remember. The following day Oscar discovered the apartments had burned to the ground overnight. There were no survivors.

From there, it was easy enough to convince him to do their bidding. He couldn't let them murder more innocent people, but he'd known they wouldn't stop with one drug. If they did it once they'd likely done it before, and would do it again. The care home in Sherman Oaks was their work, another manufactured viral outbreak. It was the fifth time in fifteen years he'd covered for their actions and helped them skirt through clinical trials.

These people know, he thought, staring with dread at the monitor. Somehow, Alexei Vasiliev and whoever he worked with knew about all of it. And worse, that same Apollo representative who'd left him with a clever quip and a knowing smirk now lay under one of the sheets, dead from internal hemorrhaging.

Quickly, before anyone else could see the document, Oscar bent with a wince to lay down his backpack and unplugged the monitor from the computer before rising again.

The game had begun.

THE MORGUE

The move was quick and obviously meant to look like he was bending over to place his backpack, but Joy noticed Oscar unplugging the monitor from the back of the grossing station computer. If she hadn't been keeping an eye on him because of his illness, whatever it was, she probably wouldn't have seen it. None of the others seemed to, in any case.

She looked away quickly as Oscar rose and turned in her direction. Clearly, he hadn't wanted anyone to see whatever was on the monitor. He'd recognized the man with his chest cracked open, but had tried to hide that, too. Was he holding back clues, hoping to save the glory for himself? She hadn't seen what had been on the screen and couldn't check for herself until he stepped away from it. What she did know was that as head virologist at Freedom Health Hospital Oscar would be very familiar with much if not all of the equipment in this room. She'd played a coroner on a short-running police procedural, and understood they were in a cross between a morgue and a pathology lab. The thing Oscar stood in front of was called a grossing station, if she recalled correctly. The screen would show magnified images of dissected organs and tissue for examination by the coroner and/or pathologist. On the series, Joy had played a smalltown coroner who also ran a local funeral home. She'd had a fondness for eating while performing autopsies, which was obviously not allowed in a real autopsy room but seemed to be a cliché in TV shows at the time. The makeup and prosthetics had been particularly realistic and she'd often found it difficult to eat, even knowing they were fake. She'd also gained ten pounds shooting those six episodes.

"Is it possible all of these people died playing the game?" Oscar said, stepping away from the station but not far enough yet for Joy to swoop in.

Henry lowered another sheet. "Like what? They were test subjects?"

"Maybe. They'd have to test the rooms, right?"

"Like beta testing," Ileana said. When the others turned to her, she shrugged. "My son's a gamer."

Rudy sneered at Jessica Danvers's feet. "Beta testing." He pronounced it *beeta*. "Did any of these people know what they were getting into, I wonder?"

"Who would *risk* that?"

Atkins sputtered. "For enough dough, people will do anything. Hell, we're living proof of that, aren't we?"

No one responded to him. They didn't need to.

During the silence, Henry bent to look at something on the side of the morgue table closest to him. "There's the same sticker on all of this equipment. Some kind of symbol with letters on it."

Rudy regarded the label. "That's the sigil of Marbas or Barbas. He's considered the Great President of Hell in *The Lesser Key of Solomon*, a demonology grimoire from the seventeenth century. Leader of thirty-six legions of demons."

"How many demons is in a legion, Doc?" Atkins said with a smirk.

Rudy wisely ignored the comment, turning instead to inspect the scales.

Joy looked closer at the grossing station. Much the equipment was labeled with the same sigil on small shiny stickers: three lines capped by small circles, joined to two three-pronged iron crosses. Letters surrounding it within a larger circle spelled out MARBAS.

"Marbas is often depicted as a lion who can change shape into a man with a lion's head. He's said to be able to change men into other shapes as well, can provide great knowledge of mechanical arts, as well as cause and heal diseases."

"A demon of medicine," Henry said.

"'*Medice, cura te ipsum*,'" Rudy said, reading the sign on the far wall. "'Physician, heal thyself.'"

With this he turned to regard Oscar, who in turn looked back at Joy. She stepped away from the grossing station, pretending to be interested in something else.

"This puzzle seems to be tailormade for you, Oscar."

"Why me?" Oscar sounded suspicious.

"You're the only one among us with a medical degree. Unless someone here has something they're not telling us."

The others shook their heads.

"Let's fan out," Henry suggested. "We need to find a way out of here before the sand and snakes show up."

Ileana pouted. "Very funny."

"There's an exit sign above the walk-in fridge," Joy said, pointing toward it. She'd noticed the walk-in right away, seeing as it was the only thing that remained of the original kitchen. Although, she noted, it had been moved to stand in front of where the door to the servants' quarters used to be in what had remained of the original house. The exit sign was new.

Henry tried the door. "It's locked." He pulled harder, placing one foot on the base of it for leverage. "Looks like we'll need a key."

"No shit," Atkins grunted.

"These scales are branded 'Merchant.'" Rudy said, one hand absently stroking his beard while he stood over the counter. "A clue, perhaps?"

Joy left the grossing station—Oscar was still hovering around it anyway, deep in thought, rubbing his lower back—and approached the counter with the scales. She noticed a drawer below it with no handle. She pushed on it, felt around the edges for some kind of hold, but found nothing. Then she looked at the manufacturer label on the front of the scale. MERCHANT was written across the top, just as Rudy had said. Below was a string of numbers and a barcode, which she supposed could be a code of some sort. Under the barcode were the words MADE IN VENICE.

She thought about it a moment. The scales, the X-rays, the locked drawer, the label. Something about these things together was on the verge of clicking...

"*The Merchant of Venice!*"

"Ahhh," Rudy said, giving her an impressed grin. "Very clever."

"What's that?" Henry asked, approaching them.

"Our resident thespian interpreted a clue."

Joy looked closer at the X-ray displays. The one on the left had what she thought was its appendix circled. The one on the right, a circle around a shadow in its brain. The center display, directly above the scale, remained empty. "Shylock required a pound of flesh," Joy said.

Ileana came over with a scowl. "Isn't he an antisemitic stereotype?"

"I don't think that's the point. I think we have to put something on the scale that weighs a pound to open this drawer."

"A pound of flesh," Oscar repeated, looking even more ill than before.

"Push on it," Ileana suggested with a nod.

Joy gave her a suspicious look. "Why don't you?"

"Fine." Ileana brushed past her and put a hand on the scale without hesitation. The other side rose, the numbers shooting up several pounds. She got it close to a pound at 1.1, then .9, but it kept fluctuating between the two and wouldn't settle.

"It has to weigh exactly a pound. What weighs exactly a pound?"

"Pound cake?" Atkins said.

Ileana snorted. "It's called that because it uses a pound of each ingredient, dimwit. Not because of its weight."

"Do I look like a baker to you?"

Joy slipped her phone out of her pocket and delicately placed it on the scale. The other side rose only slightly, the numbers settling on .63. "Anyone have a bigger phone?"

"The clue is a pound of flesh," Henry said. "The X-rays make me think that's probably important."

Rudy raised an eyebrow. "Certainly none of us is going to sever our extremities to get the key, are we?"

The others chuckled. All but Oscar, who let out a moan, still standing by the grossing station.

Ileana rose on the toes of her heels to get a better look at the top of the scale. "There's something stamped into the metal on the right side. It looks like..."

Joy joined her. "What?" She looked at it herself. It was an image of a human body lying flat inside a rectangle.

"Is that a coffin?" Ileana asked.

Joy turned back to the morgue tables, looking at the empty one. "I think one of us has to get on that table. If we do that while pressing on the scale, I think it'll trigger the mechanism."

"I'll do it," Henry said. He reached out with his left foot and touched the base of the table. When that caused no reaction, he touched the tabletop with the tips of his fingers, then pressed the hand firmly on the metallic surface. "Here goes nothing. One of you needs to be ready on the scale."

"On it," Ileana said.

Henry's shackles jingled as he climbed up onto the table, knees first, then moved around and lay back with his head against the sheet like a pillow.

Ileana pressed on the scale.

After a moment, she said, "Nothing happened."

Except that wasn't true, exactly. Overhead, the forced air came on. Joy looked up to see little pieces of crepe paper taped to the two air ducts start fluttering.

"Was that us?" Henry said, looking up from the table with concern.

"Probably just a coincidence," Ileana said, still pressing her palm on the scale. "Why would they make a puzzle that triggers the air conditioning?"

Joy stepped under the closest vent, near the slab Jessica

Danvers lay on. She raised a hand toward it but it wasn't necessary. It was like standing under a salon hair dryer. "It's not air conditioning. It's *heat*."

One thing no one had noticed when they'd been fanning out across the room was the temperature gauge on the walk-in. Joy crossed to it now. Though it normally would have displayed the temperature inside the fridge, the red needle moved visibly toward the right, already nearing seventy-five degrees. When they'd entered it had felt like normal room temperature, around seventy degrees.

"It's hot as shit in here," Atkins said. "I'm gonna be swimming in my trunks in a minute."

"There's an image," Rudy quipped.

Within seconds the temperature rose above eighty, heat blasting from several vents. Joy wiped away sweat from her upper lip. "Get off the table," she said anxiously. "Take your hand off the scale."

Henry climbed off the table. Ileana took her hand off the scale. But the air continued humming out of the vents. The little fluttering pieces of crepe paper all burst into flames at once, like birthday candles blown out in reverse.

"So much for snakes and sand," Henry said. "We need to figure this out. *Now*."

Atkins sputtered. "You don't say."

Joy hurried across the room, skirting the morgue tables to the grossing station. Oscar eyed her with suspicion as she neared. When she bent to find the cable, he asked, "What are you doing?" in a nervous tone.

"You saw something on the monitor. I need to see what it was."

"It was nothing. Forget it."

The others came over. Joy ignored Oscar's suggestion, looking for the port to plug the monitor into. "Which one of these does it plug into?"

He looked down at her with a hopeless expression, sweat glistening on his brow. Already she could feel her antiperspirant failing. The temperature was likely over ninety degrees now, with no sign of stopping any time soon. Not unless they solved this puzzle.

"*We're all gonna burn to death in this room if you don't help me, Oscar.*"

He sighed. "That one," he said, pointing it out.

Joy plugged in the monitor and stood to look at the screen. It displayed an image of a dark-red organ. Text beneath it said, ORGAN SPECIMEN, 1 LB. Oscar startled. Sweat dripped off his brow.

"What is that?" Joy asked. "A liver?"

"It's a bladder," Oscar said. "I know what we have to do." He stalked away, moving toward the empty table. He climbed up onto it with a moan of pain, flipped over and lay down. "Bring over the surgical tray."

"What are you doing?" Ileana said.

"Trust me. Joy, please bring over the tray."

Joy reached for the surgical tray from the grossing station. She hesitated. "What are we doing, Oscar?"

"You have to remove my bladder."

"Are you fucking kidding me?" Atkins grunted. The armpits of his uniform were soaked through with sweat. Same with Henry's. Ileana fanned herself with a kerchief. Rudy had taken off his ascot and was doing the same.

"I have cancer," Oscar said, sitting up. He pointed at the grossing station, where Joy still stood, still hesitating with her hand hovering above the tray. "*That thing* says we need to put my bladder on the scale."

Joy shook her head. "It might not be…"

"It is, Joy. I'm sorry but it is. You said yourself, we'll all burn to death if I don't help." He offered a sad smile. "This is me helping. Please. Bring the tray."

"Surely you can't be serious," Rudy said, his silver eyebrows furrowed in concern. "None of us are qualified to remove your bladder—"

"I'll do it myself. Joy can help me."

"I've never…" She shook her head again. "I'm not a doctor."

Oscar smiled again, this time more hopeful. "But you played one on TV."

"That's not the same," she said, her voice sounding very

small in her own ears.

"Fuck it, I'll do it," Atkins said with a decisive nod. He held out a hand. "Give me the scalpel."

Oscar gave Joy a pleading look. He clearly didn't trust anyone cutting into him but her.

"Okay," she said. She picked up the tray and brought it to the table. Oscar lay back, his head on the folded sheet. The sheet immediately became damp from the sweat in his hair.

"You're sure about this?"

"It's the only way."

Joy found herself turning to Henry for guidance. The man merely shrugged.

"Okay. Should I wash up first?"

"There's no time." Oscar pulled up his shirt. His belly was somewhat distended around the navel. "Just… soak one of the cotton balls in iodine and clean the area."

She looked again at the area right above his belt buckle. "There's a lot of hair."

"It'll be fine."

"It's ninety-eight fucking degrees, guys," Ileana said, standing at the walk-in fridge. "Whatever we're doing here has to get done fast or this metal will be too hot to touch."

"Okay…" Joy picked up the bottle of iodine. She unscrewed the cap and tilted it over a cotton ball until the white fiber turned brown. Then she swabbed the area delicately, wiping it over his olive-toned skin until it was the same yellow-brown as her fingers holding the cotton ball.

"Now the scalpel," Oscar said.

She reached for it.

"Wait!"

"What?"

"The hypo. What does it say?"

She looked at the small label. "Um… it says Marbas."

"Anything besides that?"

"'Nerve block.'"

He nodded. "Okay. Inject that right here," he said, pointing to a spot right above his groin.

"You're sure."

"We don't have time to second guess, Dr. Margaret."

The sound of her character's name eased the tension somewhat. She nodded and picked up the syringe. Already her fingers were slick with sweat. She thought about how difficult it would be to cut him open with slippery fingers and tried to push it from her mind. It wasn't helpful.

"Dr. Margaret...?" Rudy wondered aloud.

Henry held up a hand to silence him.

You're a surgeon, Joy thought, trying to convince her mind that what she was about to do was not only the right thing but also the only choice available. This wasn't just Method acting, a practice some of her more prestigious colleagues claimed to follow. Right here in this moment, she *was* a surgeon. She would *have* to be.

Still, she hesitated a moment with the needle hovering over his groin.

"It's okay," Oscar said.

Henry nodded. "You can do this," he said.

"What if something happens? These people..." She nodded toward the morgue tables. "...they must have done the same thing we're doing, right?"

"Maybe. But I know for sure at least one of them didn't have medical training. It's possible the others didn't either."

"How do you—?" She stopped herself. It didn't matter how he knew. He could've just been lying to boost her confidence. "Okay," she said a third time, then plunged the needle into the hard paunch above his belt and depressed the plunger before she could think better of it.

"Henry, grab the sheet from under my head and get ready to swab up the blood. There's gonna be a lot of it."

Oscar raised his head as Henry reached for the sheet, but Atkins slapped Henry's hand before he could grab it. "I'll do it," he said, and picked up the sheet himself.

It was clear Oscar didn't trust Atkins, but he couldn't exactly back out now. "All right. Now, pick up the scalpel."

Joy did. Her fingers were still slick but she gripped it the way the medical consultant had taught her during the series, like a pencil with her middle finger further up the handle. Six years later, she still remembered.

"Rest the tip of the blade right here," Oscar said, pointing. She followed his instruction. "Now when you make the incision, move your arm not your hand."

"I remember," Joy said. She inhaled deeply, exhaling as she pressed the blade into his flesh until blood rose to the surface.

"Don't worry. I can't feel a thing."

She nodded and drew her arm back, dragging the blade, the flesh parting like the red sea—a literal red sea pouring out of him. Atkins followed her movement with the sheet. The white fabric soaked up Oscar's blood hungrily.

"That should be good," Oscar said.

"One hundred and five," Ileana called over. Her hair stood out in wet frizzled curls. Rudy had taken off his coat and undone the top two buttons of his dress shirt. His armpit sweat stains had soaked into his vest.

"I feel like I might faint," he said.

"That's heat syncope," Oscar told him, surprisingly lucid despite his loss of blood. "Get some cool water from the grossing station sink and soak your ascot, then hold it on your forehead."

Rudy wobbled into action. He staggered and fell back against the counter.

"I'll do it," Henry said.

Atkins glared at him.

"You've got your hands full already," Henry reminded him.

Atkins nodded.

"Joy," Oscar said. "Are you with me?"

She nodded.

Henry took Rudy's coat and ascot and brought them to the sink.

"You'll have to sort of pry open the incision. Can you do that?"

"I think so." The incision lay open like parted lips as Atkins swabbed it with the sheet, soaking up the blood. Joy reached in with her other hand and parted it further, revealing the insides of his abdomen, all orange-yellow fatty tissue and pink and dark red organs, spiderwebbed with thick red veins.

"There's no water," Henry said. "The tap doesn't work."

"I'll be... fine," Rudy said, leaning against the counter with a glazed look to his eyes. He didn't look fine but it was obvious he couldn't act as though he was dying when a man was lying on a table in front of him having literal surgery under local anesthetic.

"Are you still with me?" Oscar said.

"I'm here."

"You see the flat organ right near the front, darker than the rest and sort of shaped like a manta ray?"

"I see it."

"Okay, I want you to reach in and tug it out, as gently as you can."

"Jesus," Atkins grunted.

Joy didn't hesitate this time. Holding open the incision with her left hand, she reached into the abdominal cavity, slipping the fingers of her right under what she assumed by Oscar's own description was his bladder. Very gently she started tugging it away from the other organs and fatty tissue, the yellow fat stretching but still attached to the organ, looking something like wet cheese cloth. The organ itself was riddled with large bumpy cysts.

Cancer, she thought. *The most terrifying demon of all.*

Finally, she was able to pull the deathly organ partway out of him, tugging on three long fleshy tubes, two from the top, which she assumed connected to his kidneys, one from below to his urethra. She couldn't imagine how he must be feeling in this moment, watching himself being massacred, *participating* in it. She just hoped they were able to get it out without killing him.

People did survive this surgery every day. Surgeons put in a stoma to attach a urostomy bag and patients were out in a few days.

But Joy wasn't a real surgeon, as badly as she wanted to pretend she was in this moment. These weren't normal circumstances and this wasn't a sterile environment. If anything, it was downright *hostile*, like a combat hospital under heavy fire.

"Henry," Oscar called.

"Yeah." Henry's voice right behind Joy startled her. In her intense focus on Oscar's inner workings, she hadn't even noticed the man's approach.

"I need you to hold me up," Oscar said. His voice was fading. His eyelids fluttered. His face was ashen. It made sense that someone would have to raise him. The muscles in his abdominal wall had been severed. He couldn't exactly lift himself.

Henry said nothing, moving swiftly around the table behind Atkins—who eyed him as he passed, still holding the sheet against Oscar's incision, mopping up blood—and stopping beside Oscar. Henry set down the book and slid one hand under Oscar's shoulders, the other under his head. Both men were drenched in sweat.

"Careful," Oscar said.

Henry gently lifted Oscar to a sitting position.

"One hundred and seven," Ileana said, her voice weak. Her hair had come entirely loose from its high-up style and hung in sweaty clumps over her bare, sweat-slicked shoulders. Her face was flushed.

How hot until we boil internally? Joy wondered.

As if sensing her thoughts, Oscar said, "The human body can stand up to... one hundred and eight... depending on humidity. We still have time... but not much." His words were piecemeal now, spoken between breaths. He looked down at himself, blood still spilling from the wound, soaked up by the towel. "I can take it... from here." He held out a hand. "Hand me the scalpel."

Joy's hands were occupied, holding both the incision and the bladder. Atkins took one hand off the sheet to pick up the scalpel and pass it, handle forward, to Oscar.

"Thank you," Oscar said. His voice was getting weaker by the second. Joy wasn't sure he'd survive much more of this. He needed water and fresh blood and IV fluid. The heat was nearly enough to kill a healthy person, let alone someone with an eight-inch incision in their abdomen.

"Hold it up, please, Joy. You're doing fine."

93

"How are *you* doing?"

He flashed a smile. "Never better. You see those... little clips... on the tray?"

Joy saw them. She nodded.

"I need you to... put them on each ureter, about an inch... above the bladder. Can you..." He swallowed audibly. "...do that?"

Still holding the bladder outside of his body, she let go of the incision and grabbed the first of the clips, whose names she'd probably learned during shooting but couldn't recall now. She slid it over the slender, fleshy tube on Oscar's right side, snapping it closed, then did the same on the left. Oscar didn't react, so the local anesthetic was clearly doing its job.

"Good," he said. "Now hold it... steady. I'm going to make... the first cut."

With expert precision he drew the blade across the right ureter. It snapped free and wriggled like a worm cut in half by a shovel blade. A few dribbles of blood leaked out into Oscar's gut.

Joy glanced over at the next table, where the man with his chest cracked open lay under a white sheet. She'd wanted to ask Oscar how he knew the man, but now was clearly not the time.

As if alerted by her thoughts, the dead man's right arm jumped off the table, slipped out from under the sheet and hung loose over the side. Oscar said, "Oops."

"What?" she asked urgently, but she quickly learned the answer herself. Dark urine poured out of the gash into his abdominal cavity. As the amber liquid spilled over her hand, she noticed it was cooler than her skin, almost soothingly so.

The room is hotter than body temperature, she thought abstractly.

"I nicked... the bladder."

"Is that bad?"

He nodded slightly. "Infection... is likely. I never... expected to... survive this... anyway."

"We have to do something," she said.

"One-hundred and nine," Ileana said, her voice raspy.

"Joy..." Oscar said, barely above a whisper.

She took his hand. He squeezed lightly.

"You beat this... son of a bitch."

Joy nodded. A tear spilled down her cheek. "We will."

With one final cut Oscar freed the bladder and the deflating organ fell into the palm of Joy's hand like a dead sea creature. Atkins snatched it up, dropping the towel. He hurried to the scale. Henry laid Oscar down gently.

Vaguely, she heard a sharp click and the sound of wood sliding against wood to her left. "Got it," Atkins called. She saw him run behind Oscar in a blur toward the fridge. Joy held Oscar's gaze.

"Hurry!" Ileana said.

The key rattled against the lock.

"This is like... that scene..." His dazed eyes struggled to remain focused. The pupils had nearly swallowed up the entirety of his warm amber irises. "...with Dr. Margaret..."

Joy nodded, remembering the one he was referencing. Her tears then had been faked. They were real now.

"I just wanted..." Another dry click as he swallowed. "...to be part of the team..."

His eyes widened suddenly, staring up at the ceiling as if he'd witnessed something profound... or profoundly terrifying. Then the life left them as his lungs expelled his final breath.

THE RULES

JOY, WE HAVE to go!" Henry shouted, holding open the door.

"Move it or lose it, woman!" Ileana whispered hoarsely behind him.

Cool air poured out over Henry in a mist as Joy took one last look at Oscar, lying dead on the slab. The temperature in this cramped corrugated metal vestibule was shockingly cool compared to the pathology lab. He'd almost fainted from the change and had to lean against the wall until his vision came back.

Joy hurried through the door into the darkened walk-in. Atkins yanked the door shut before the heat could fill the room. As he did, a door behind Henry and the others came open.

Rudy leaned against the doorway, wiping condensation from his glasses with the sleeve of his shirt, looking back at them with bleary eyes. "What will happen to the bodies?" he asked.

Henry hummed. "At a guess? They'll be cremated."

"Jesus," Atkins muttered.

Henry slipped the key he'd snatched from the fridge lock into his back pocket while Atkins wasn't looking. He didn't know if it would be useful in the future, but living in a cell for almost two years had ingrained in him that keys were all important. Keys meant *freedom*.

"You gonna be okay?" Henry asked Joy, watching her wipe away tears as she leaned her back against the door.

She nodded, sniffling. "I think so." Shaking her head, she

said, "Probably not. Why did he make me do that?"

"If you didn't, we'd all be cooking to death in that room. He sacrificed himself so we could keep going."

"Guys?" Ileana said, her voice still a raspy whisper.

He turned to see her pushing open the newly unlocked door. Beyond was what looked like a TV studio, darkened seating filled with a crowd of people, an area for two studio cameras, and what looked like a brightly lit daytime talk-show set: two long, curved sofas in front of a coffee table, a cityscape seen between tall wooden panels, and a large monitor, about the same size as the one Oscar and Joy had cracked in the foyer.

Was this whole thing some psycho's idea of a reality game show? Are they taping this right now?

A single word in a foreign language—Greek, from the look—faded in and out in various spots on the TV screen, written as though it was a signature:

"Any idea what that means?" Henry asked.

Rudy blinked at the foreign script. "Achlys. The Greek goddess of Eternal Night."

"Oh, thank God!" Ileana gasped, a few steps inside the studio. She hurried to a water cooler against the wall near the door, tore a paper cup from the dispenser, filled it, and drank the water in two swift gulps.

"Goddess of poison," Rudy finished absently, his gaze falling on Ileana, who'd already begun pouring another cup full of water.

"Guys, it's cold," she said. "Ohmigod, it's *so good.*"

Rudy slapped the cup out of her hand. Water splashed over her dress but she was already drenched with sweat.

"What the fuck did you do that for?"

"Achlys is the goddess of *poison*," Rudy told her.

"Oh, shit. Oh, fuck." She started pacing, like she had in the foyer. "Fuck, fuck, fuck!"

The water cooler glubbed innocently.

On the large screen Henry noticed the logo fade to black

before a shot of the set took its place, accompanied by an instrumental version of a cheery 80s pop song Henry couldn't quite place. An APPLAUSE sign high above the set flashed red and cheers erupted. The sound appeared to be coming from the studio audience, but not a single person in the chairs moved. And though the set was empty but for the décor, on the screen Alexei Vasiliev sat on the sofa on stage right, wearing a well-tailored suit and a big phony smile.

Ileana groaned from the shadows behind them. "Is that 'Don't Stop Thinking About Tomorrow'?" she asked with distaste.

"It's just called 'Don't Stop,'" Joy told her.

"Welcome back to the show," their host said with faux cheer. "If you've just joined us, we were last speaking with Dr. Oscar Evans, who sacrificed his life to save his newfound friends. Let's give a great big round of applause for Oscar, yes, folks?"

More applause arose from the crowd, the exact same sound as the last. *Canned*, they used to call it. Henry had once read that TV shows still used laughter and applause that was recorded decades ago, and that many of the people heard in those recordings were likely dead. He didn't know if it was true but it made the scene before him even more chilling, looking over the unmoving heads and shoulders of what was likely an audience of mannequins.

"Thank you," Alexei said with a fake smile. "Wow, what a rush, yes? You can *feel* the adrenaline pumping through your veins, can't you?" He thumped his chest for dramatic effect as he spoke. "Almost like a poison."

"Fuck!" Ileana said again. She shoved two fingers into her mouth and gagged but nothing came up.

"Yes, the water the more reckless of you have just consumed to quench your no doubt powerful thirst is laced with an extremely deadly poison and you will be dead within approximately ten minutes, *unless*..." He raised a finger at this. "Unless, my friends, you find the antidote."

The motionless audience *ooooh*ed.

"I'm gonna die," Ileana moaned. "I'm gonna die. God, why

can't I *throw up*?"

"You know what? Why don't we make this a little more interesting? If you don't find the antidote—or the exit—within ten minutes, the studio will be flooded with carbon monoxide and every one of you will die. Ironic, isn't it, that the very air which we exhale is a single molecule away from killing us? We'll be right back after these important messages from our sponsors."

Applause filled the studio again as the shot faded to black, leaving a countdown in its place.

09:59:59...

:58...

:57

"He's not half as clever as he thinks he is," Rudy muttered, still panting against the wall.

"That doesn't sound like him," Joy said. "Alexei wasn't like that. I won't say he was *kind* but... He was sadist, like you said, especially after he got involved with Infiniti. But he wasn't *gleefully* sadistic. It was..." She shook her head, as if trying not to recall hurtful details. "It was almost as if he was regretful for what he'd done, when he did it, if that makes sense. Like it wasn't something he wanted to do, more like—"

"He was *compelled*?" Rudy suggested.

Joy nodded. "Exactly."

Atkins let out a barked laugh. "Well, he's a far cry from that now, huh?"

Henry was only half paying attention to the others. His mind had stuck on what Joy had said about Infiniti. It was the second time he'd heard the name today, but not the only time he'd heard it in his life. It had come up before, when he was looking into a suspicious apartment fire in Long Beach. Must've been fourteen or fifteen years ago. They'd pinned the job on a local firebug who'd been burning up empty buildings as some ass-backwards protest against urban sprawl, but it later came to light that Infiniti Enterprises, whoever they were, had been trying to buy up the land for an ultra-modern development— which they were able to do shortly after the fire was swept under the carpet. The Juno Tower stood there now, towering over every other building in the area aside from the recently completed Shoreline Gateway, which was only a few feet taller. Juno was a mixed space of condos and offices now, and also happened to be home to the mysterious Infiniti Enterprises itself.

"All right, let's get moving," Henry said, allowing these memories of his previous life to fade into the background. Whatever part Infiniti played in what was happening here, solving this damned puzzle and getting Ileana her antidote was far more important at the moment.

Rudy pushed himself off the wall with a tired grunt. "This set... it looks familiar."

"It's the Janice Staudenmaier set," Joy said as the four of them headed down the center aisle, between rows and rows of male and female mannequins in various outfits, staring blank-eyed at the stage. "I did one of my first interviews—" She stopped there, staring down at the set with her mouth open.

"Your first interviews...?" Rudy prodded.

"Nothing," Joy said.

"Who were the other guests that day?" Henry asked, taking a different approach, the way he'd often tried to jog the memories of victims who'd forgotten the details of crimes either consciously or not.

"It was Chris Hemsworth and myself. We were on a promo tour for our new movie."

"Anyone else?"

She considered it. "A celebrity chef. I don't remember her name. And some writer. A biographer, I think."

"What did she cook? Do you remember?"

"Oh, it was this amazing chocolate soufflé."

"Hemsworth... that's the guy who plays Thor, right?"

"Lucky bitch got to kiss him," Ileana called over, apparently able to ignore her impending death for a moment to tend to her jealousy.

"If you're not experiencing any symptoms, we're gonna need your help over here," Henry said to her. "I realize you're scared right now, but the more heads the better."

"Fuck you, okay? I've got ten minutes to live."

"So do the rest of us, if we don't find a way out," Rudy reminded her.

"*Fine.*" She stopped her pacing and started following the wall to the left of them, looking for an exit.

Henry squeezed Rudy's shoulder. The man looked like he might pass out if he didn't stay focused. "Tell us about Achlys."

"Yes," Rudy said with a nod. "Achlys is thought to be the first created being in some ancient Greek cosmogonies, even before Chaos. She's the goddess of eternal night, representing misery and sadness."

Atkins grabbed one of the mannequins out of its chair by the shoulders. "Ugly fucks, aren't they?" He tossed it into the aisle where it sprawled with a clatter of plastic.

Joy scowled at him. "Was that necessary?"

"Just making sure they're not alive."

The thought seemed to spark fear in Joy, and she spun around to take in the entire mannequin audience. "There was a giveaway that day," she said.

"What was it?"

"Under the chairs." Joy dropped down to her hands and knees, peering into the shadows under the seats, between pants and shoes and plastic ankles. After a moment she seemed to spot something and sprung to her feet. As she neared the aisle, the entire audience of mannequins turned their heads to face her with a clattering racket, the ones in the rows ahead of her twisting all the way around like that kid in the *Exorcist* movie.

"Jeeeezus," Atkins muttered.

Joy paused briefly, glancing up at the countdown on the monitor. With no other choice she sidled down an aisle, peering cautiously back and forth at the frozen faces on either side of her as their heads turned to track her progress. She stopped near the middle, eyeing the male mannequin in the seat before her. When she crouched, watching its featureless face as she reached under one of the seats, Henry expected the thing to reach out and grab her. He imagined the whole audience of them getting up out of their seats and piling on her, tearing her limb from limb. The image was surprisingly vivid, almost like a premonition.

But the mannequins remained motionless, and Joy rose a moment later with a small white box.

"What is it?" Rudy asked.

"Maybe it's a soufflé," Atkins said with a laugh.

No one joined him.

Joy returned to them, the heads following her progress as she moved sideways quickly down the aisle. Once she returned to the others, the heads flipped back around to face the front.

"Well, that was creepy," she said, out of breath. She'd been through the ringer lately, and both the cakebox and her hands proved it, smeared and crusted with Oscar's blood.

"You open it," she said to Rudy.

Rudy peeled off the tape and lifted the lid. "Oh my," he said.

"What? What is it?" Ileana called over, making her way to the back of the set.

"It's a gas mask," Henry said, guessing without having seen it.

Rudy pulled it out of the box and regarded the thing sickly, the straps hanging limply. "Was there anything else under the seats, Joy?"

She shook her head somberly. "Just that. At least that I could see."

"Great," Atkins said. "So who gets to wear the only thing that'll save our lives if we don't fucking solve this in time?"

"We'll decide that if it comes to it," Henry replied. He looked at the timer on the screen. "We've still got almost eight minutes. I suggest we make the best of it." They all nodded and followed him to the set. "Tell us more about Achlys," he said as he mounted the stage.

Rudy nodded, looking over objects as they spread out across the set. "Right. In Hesiod's epic poem *Shield of Heracles*, she's depicted as pale and emaciated, weeping blood. 'By them stood Achlys, mournful and fearful, pale, shrunk with hunger and swollen-kneed. Long nails on her fingers, and she dribbled from the nose, and from her cheeks blood dripped to the ground. She stood leering hideously, and much dust sodden with tears lay upon her shoulders.' I can't recall the text verbatim, but it's something along those lines."

Atkins shook his head, tossing a pillow off the sofa. "How exactly does that help us?"

"We'll know that soon enough, won't we?"

Rather than reply, Atkins tossed the remaining couch cushions onto the floor.

Henry looked up at the clock. Just under seven minutes left. He crossed to the back wall of the set, inspecting the tall print of the cityscape, running his hands over the fake wood panels, looking for give. Joy approached him with a conspiratorial look.

"I think Oscar knew one of the bodies in the morgue," she whispered.

Henry nodded. "Yeah, I heard that, too."

"What does that mean?"

"Maybe nothing." He gave her a pointed look. "Maybe everything. What city is this?" he said at a volume for the others to hear.

"Looks like Akron, Ohio!" Ileana called from behind the set. "Guys, I found a door! It's locked!"

"No shit," Atkins muttered, shaking his head in derision as he moved toward one of the potted plants.

"*Janice* was shot in Burbank, not Akron," Joy said.

"And there's some weird plexiglass-looking box back here, too!" Ileana said. "It's got a door in it!"

Joy's face alighted with recognition. "There was a contest that day. One of those cash-in-a-box things."

"I hate that," Henry said. "Just give them the damn money."

"Right? That has to be relevant."

"The door's locked on this thing too," Ileana shouted, "but it's got a hole for a key!"

"Akron is Greek," Rudy said, digging his hands into the folds of the couch as if searching for a lost remote control. "It means summit, or high point."

"Ileana, look against the walls," Henry called out. "Can you see a ladder?"

"Nope! Wait, yeah! Not sure where it leads, it's pretty dark up there and there's a light shining right in my eyes!"

"That's gotta be our exit," Joy said excitedly.

She and Henry both turned to the timer as it dropped below six minutes.

Henry resumed looking over the set. There was a lot of ground to cover for something as small as a key. But he had a key in his pocket, didn't he? The Book, too. He still had that, however useful or worthless it might become.

He was about to head to the back to join Ileana when he noticed Rudy frowning at Atkins, who brushed his fingers through the fake ferns and moved onward. Rudy approached the pot just as Atkins left it.

"There's a label on this planter," he said, scowling again at the back of Atkins's head. "'Do not ingest. Highly toxic.'"

"Sounds like our goddess, doesn't it?" Henry said.

"Indeed." Rudy pulled up his sleeve and reached in between the long stems of the fake plastic fern. He dug around for a moment, then his thick eyebrows rose. A moment later his hand emerged, holding something shiny between thumb and forefinger. "Our key," he said.

They all met at stage right. Henry glanced at the timer, which dipped below five minutes and thirty seconds, then headed around the set to the darkened backstage. The others followed him. He heard beeps and looked back to see Atkins setting his watch.

"Good thinking."

Atkins shrugged. "First time I've used it. Figured it's gotta be good for something."

Backstage was littered with sandbags and lights and cables. Ileana stood in front of a plexiglass box which appeared to be welded to the floor, spotlighted by a light in the catwalks above them. Unlike the previous room an exit sign didn't accompany the door she'd mentioned, on the opposite side of the box. The ladder, closer to them, rose into the darkness.

"There's something attached to the ceiling of this," Ileana said, peering up into the box with a hand shielding her eyes. "I can't tell what it is with that stupid fucking light shining in my face."

"How are you feeling?" Henry asked as he and the others

approached the box.

"I'm okay." Ileana nodded. She looked frazzled but no worse than the rest of them. "No symptoms yet."

"Good. We're gonna find that antidote."

She nodded again, looking like she didn't buy it, aware it was a platitude.

Rudy was looking up into the rafters with a pair of clip-in shades over his glasses. "There's an exit sign up there," he said, pointing to where the ladder entered the shadows. "Along with what appears to be a hatch of some sort."

"The key, Rudy," Henry prodded.

"Yes, of course," the professor said, removing the clip-ons and tucking them into his breast pocket. Rather than unlock the door himself, he held the key out to Henry. Henry fought back a grin as he took it. Despite the obvious handicap of being the only one in chains, he'd somehow fallen into the role of leader. The guys at the station might've chuckled knowingly if they'd seen it—or they would have, prior to what he'd done. None of them had stuck with him after that, not even his partner. He'd been a groomsman at her wedding and godfather to her son. Not even as much as a postcard in two years.

And who could blame any of them? How could a cop trust someone who'd shot and killed one of their own?

Henry tucked the Book under his left arm and unlocked the door. It opened with a sucking sound like a refrigerator door, but stopped after about a foot, prevented from opening further by an unseen force. Maybe the hinges were only meant to open just so far. Whatever the reason, it would make retrieving the black leather pouch taped to the ceiling difficult. He stuck his arm in up to the shoulder, but his reach was about six inches too short and a few inches shy laterally. As he removed his arm, he noticed a rectangular flap above the door. It reminded him of the food slot in the doors in solitary confinement. He pushed it. Like the door it had some kind of magnetic suction to it, but it opened easily enough, then snapped shut when he let it go.

Air-tight? he thought, then wondered why he'd asked himself that. The answer troubled him.

"What's that symbol on it?" Joy asked.

Henry hadn't noticed a symbol, but squinting up again he saw something white printed on the bottom of the pouch.

Rudy stepped to the other side of the booth, looking up at it with the gas mask hanging from a hand at his side. "The Staff of Asclepius," he said. "The original symbol for medicine and healing. One might say the mortal enemy of our Achlys."

"The antidote!" Ileana cried.

"Someone's gonna need to squeeze in there and get it," Henry said, leaving the rest of the thought unspoken.

Joy seemed to take his cue. "You think it's a trap?"

"Judging by what we've seen so far, I'd say it's unlikely *not* to be a trap."

Ileana squeezed between Joy and Atkins to Henry's side. "I'll do it."

"What if it is a trap?"

She shrugged. "I'm the asshole who drank the poison. If that's the antidote, I should be the one to get it."

"It's too high," Joy said. "She'll never reach it."

"I'm a climber." Henry caught Joy's reaction to this: she was clearly remembering Ileana's horrific escape from the Egyptian room, climbing over the convulsing body of her companion. "I've free soloed out of crevasses wider than this. I can do it."

"A woman of many talents, surely," Rudy said, wiping his glasses on his sleeve. "However, I do think *something* might prevent you from… making entry."

Ileana sputtered laughter. "Are you talking about my ass?"

"I can squeeze through," Joy said.

"Listen, you skinny bitch, it's *my* antidote. I should be the one to—"

"Four and a half minutes," Atkins grunted, looking at his watch.

Henry eyed her, impressing upon her the weight of her decision. "Can you climb?"

She held his gaze a moment, then shrugged and shook her head. "Maybe."

"I can reach it," Rudy said. He stepped out from behind the box. "And I believe I might be just svelte enough to sidle through." Without giving anyone a chance to argue, he stepped in front of the opening and thrust the gas mask toward Joy. "Take this, would you?"

Joy did, holding it to her chest.

Henry threw an arm across the opening. "You don't have to do this."

Rudy gave him a tight smile. It was clear he knew exactly what Henry was thinking: that this was very clearly a trap, that the box might not be airtight, that whoever remained inside it would likely die without the gas mask, that all of them might die if no one retrieved the antidote, and Ileana would *certainly* die without it. Did he know Henry was also wondering what they'd do if he died, leaving them with little to no knowledge of gods and demons? Did Rudy know he was wondering how they'd survive? "We can argue it for the next four minutes, if you like?" was all Rudy said in response.

Henry held his gaze, then let go of the door jam.

"Right then." Rudy sidled up to the opening. Henry held the door, ready if the mechanism tried to pull it shut. "Here we *go*." Sucking in his stomach, Rudy squeezed through the opening.

Surprisingly, the door didn't even budge in Henry's grip. Everyone let out a sigh along with Rudy's exhaled laughter as he turned to face them.

"All that pomp and circumstance for naught," he said with a grin. "Now, let's get that antidote." He stretched to grab for the pouch. For one moment Henry was sure he'd be unable to reach it and this would've all been for nothing. But his fingers were as long and slender as his body. He grasped it and pulled it down. "Here we are—"

The door jerked roughly, pulling Henry forward. His chains rattled. "Atkins!" he called.

Atkins reached past him and grabbed the door. Joy came at it from the front, pushing.

Henry saw the look on Rudy's face, the clear sense of impending doom. But rather than help push at the door, the man bent swiftly and tossed the pouch through the opening.

Then the door tore free of their grip and Joy leaped back as it slammed shut.

Ileana scooped up the pouch from the floor and quickly

unzipped it.

"Bugger," Rudy said. "Tell me it was worth my while, Ileana."

"It's here," she said, pulling out a hypo from inside. She pulled off the stopper with her teeth. "Where do I stick it?"

"I'd suggest the upper arm or thigh."

Ileana nodded, staring at the needle. "Can someone do it for me? I'm, uh… I'm kind of afraid of needles."

"Give it to me," Joy said, clearly annoyed. She passed the gas mask to Atkins. Ileana gave her a wary look as she neared, then handed over the syringe.

"May I see the Book, Henry?" Rudy asked. "The next two pages. Just out of curiosity."

Behind him, Ileana sucked in a pained breath. "You did that on purpose, didn't you?"

"If you keep squirming it'll happen again. Stay still."

"*Fine.*"

Henry opened the book. He flipped past the images of Apep the sun-eating demon to find the following two pages had filled with intricate drawings and script of their own. He turned it toward the booth and held it up against the plexiglass.

"*Ow!*" Ileana said behind him.

Rudy's eyes widened in awe as he studied the images. "Just as I suspected. The Book in your hands is an ancient grimoire, much older than the Christian Bible. Whispered about in theological circles. A Book of magic, but also a *magic Book*. It contains rituals meant to open a portal to realms beyond the human imagination to comprehend."

"Rituals," Henry repeated.

Rudy held his gaze. "Requiring human sacrifice."

"Then each one of these rooms…"

The professor nodded. "I'd been researching the existence of this Book for decades. My colleagues were certain it doesn't exist. A Book predating Hinduism and Zoroastrianism, connecting all of human religion under one ethos? A unified theory of theological and demonological study? Surely just a myth."

"But books didn't exist until…" Joy began, leaving the

thought unfinished. Ileana rubbed her thigh, wincing in pain but not dead.

"Quite later, yes. The oldest papyrus was discovered dating back to 2900 B.C. The oldest *book* very much later."

"Hey, uh, this is interesting and all," Atkins said, "but we've got under three minutes."

"I only need another moment with Henry," Rudy said briskly. "Perhaps the ladies should make their way up the ladder?"

Joy and Ileana looked at one another briefly, then hurried toward it. "I'll go first," Joy said.

"You don't trust me?"

"Would you?"

"Fair."

As their footfalls began clanging up the ladder, Rudy said, "A man came to me several years ago claiming to have discovered a very old Book in an ancient burial chamber in Iraq. Perhaps the *oldest* Book. I believe it may be the very Book you're holding."

"But the pages were empty," Henry said.

"Perhaps they merely *appeared* to be empty. Perhaps the human mind isn't meant to comprehend such things."

"What are you saying?"

"I'm saying, Henry, that this Book *was not created by man*." Atkins scoffed.

"You're saying…"

"Yes, Henry. A day later I was contacted by a woman who claimed the man I spoke to was mad. She told me no such book existed and I should discontinue my search for the Al-Qiyama Codex, named after the seventy-fifth *surah* of the Quran at the time it was discovered. She gave me her card and suggested if I spoke to this man again, I should contact her immediately. That same woman lay on one of the slabs in the morgue."

Rudy reached into his back pocket and retrieved his wallet. He pulled out a business card and held it up to the glass. Henry regarded it, noticing the logo at the top, the symbol for infinity, and the name encircling it.

"Infiniti Enterprises," he said.

"Indeed. They pressured me into denouncing the man's findings and giving up my search for the Book. If we had more time, I could explain why I allowed it. Suffice to say, these are extremely powerful people and not to be trifled with, Henry. And this conspiracy goes well beyond this infernal house."

Henry let Rudy's words marinate. He'd witnessed how deeply someone could get sucked into conspiracy theories in his time on the force. It had torn the man's life apart, shredded away his sanity, and put him in an early grave.

Henry squeezed his eyes shut, the image of Clara's lifeless face as Jeb Anderson lifted the sheet in the morgue, threatening to surface. He'd replayed the scene so often in his head he could recall every aspect with total clarity. But this was not the time. He couldn't afford to get weepy.

"Open the slot," he said finally.

Rudy tucked his wallet back into his pocket, reached up and opened it.

"Atkins?"

"What?"

"Give him the gas mask."

"Are you crazy? We got less than two minutes to climb that goddamn ladder, Hall. There's no guarantee it's even a way out!"

"Atkins, goddammit, don't you get it? They *want* us to keep going! They need human sacrifices!"

"They'll get em if we don't get moving!"

"These are *rituals*, Atkins! Each puzzle is a sacrificial ritual. We solve them and one of us dies. But we don't have to play by their rules, do we? Give him the mask. The rest of us still have a chance to survive, but if he dies, I have a feeling none of that will matter."

Shaking his head, Rudy gave Atkins an imploring look.

"Fuck, fine." Atkins stomped over and dropped the gas mask through the slot. It clattered hollowly to the floor. As Rudy bent and picked it up, Atkins headed for the ladder. "I'm outta here."

Rudy pulled the straps over his head, leaving the mask resting on his crown. "God speed, Henry."

"You too."

"One fucking minute, Hall!" Atkins called, already climbing the rungs. "Move your ass!"

Henry gave Rudy one last look. As he made to leave, Rudy spoke his name, his voice hollow and muted through the gas mask.

"Yeah?"

The archeologist gave him a serious look through the eyes of the mask. "I believe your ward is working against us."

Henry spotted Atkins's shadowy form moving up the ladder. Rudy nodded gravely. Henry thanked him, then turned and ran for the ladder. He tucked the Book down the front of his pants and stepped onto the first rung.

So many thoughts circled his mind as he ascended. Firstly, how likely were they to survive subsequent rooms without Rudy's knowledge of religious history? Were they leaving their one chance to escape behind, to possibly die? And what if Rudy was right? If Atkins really was working against them, to what purpose? It wasn't as though he'd wanted to be here. In fact, he'd actively tried to get out of it. It made no sense for him to throw a wrench into their escape plans when he was just as likely to die as the rest of them.

Below them, the instrumental version of "Don't Stop" resumed and applause erupted from the audience. From here, Henry could see the top of the box but not Rudy inside it. He assumed the man had sat down, waiting it out. He could see the seats filled with mannequins over the top of the set. They were somehow even creepier from up here, their dead-eyed faces following his upward progress.

"Welcome back to the program," Alexei said from the monitor as the theme music faded away, his voice far off and tinny. "It seems time has run out for our players. What do you say? Should we let them go? Or shall we turn on the gas?"

His query was met with cheers of "*GAS! GAS! GAS!*"

"Well, it seems quite unanimous, doesn't it? Without further ado…"

A loud hiss arose from all directions as clouds of gray smoke poured from exhaust pipes along the studio walls, causing Henry to pick up his pace. He was maybe ten feet from the opening, glancing up to see Atkins climb through into whatever room lay above them, when the Book slipped from the waistband of his pants and caught against his right thigh.

"Shit!"

It was hard enough climbing with shackles on his wrists and ankles without having to deal with the possibility of losing the Book down the leg of his pants.

They'd already lost Rudy. If they lost the Book, they might as well just give up and let the gas take them.

"Come on, Henry!" Joy called down from the opening, barely ten feet above his head.

It was impossible to hold the book in place and climb the ladder with his hands in chains. He couldn't reach down to resituate it, let alone hold it in place.

"Fuck it," he muttered, hoping like hell it wouldn't slide any further down the leg of his pants as he ascended the final rungs. He kept his leg bent at the knee, reaching up as far as the chains would allow with his free leg rather than pushing up with the one holding the Book. It was difficult work but with Joy cheering him on and the sound of the gas below reminding him that death was literally at his feet, he finally managed to make it.

Atkins and Joy pulled him through the opening into a much smaller, dimly lit room. Henry reached down the front of his pants and retrieved the Book. He peered down one last time at the smog-filled studio as a thought occurred to him.

He'd forgotten to ask Rudy about Nungal.

Before he could consider shouting down to him, Atkins slammed the hatch shut.

THE SIGIL

WHAT THE FUCK is this?" Ileana said.

Joy stayed crouched in front of the trapdoor a moment with Henry at her side. It was clear they were both thinking the same thing. Joy was the first to voice it. "He'll be okay, right?"

Henry looked up from the door in the floor. "I honestly don't know."

Joy sighed. He was right, there was no way to know for sure. Even if the money booth was close to air-tight, the gas mask could've been deliberately faulty. But the puzzle hadn't been meant for Rudy. Not if it followed the same rules as the room before it. The *Janice* studio, where she'd first announced her engagement to Alexei, the water, a clear reminder of the basement room he'd trapped her in… everything about it pointed to *her*, just as everything about the previous room had been meant for Oscar. Although, if she thought about it the morgue could also have easily been meant for her as well, considering her role as Dr. Margaret.

"I think I was meant to die down there," she said.

He looked at her sidelong, the two of them still crouched in front of the trapdoor. "What makes you say that?"

Joy shrugged, not ready to reveal all of her cards just yet. "Just a hunch. The water. You know?"

Henry nodded. "No compass, though. Listen, Rudy said some things down there—"

"There's no handle on this door," Atkins said before Henry could elaborate. The corrections officer was running his hands along the doorjamb, then pounded on it in apparent frustration.

Henry opened his mouth to finish what he'd been telling her, but was interrupted again, this time by Ileana.

"Guys, what the hell? There's pictures of all of us on this board."

"What?" Atkins brushed past them as Joy and Henry stood up to get a look at their surroundings. Henry's mouth dropped open.

"What the fuck *is* this?" he said, echoing Ileana's words.

They stood in what appeared to be the office of a paranoid schizophrenic. The desk was cluttered with documents, opened file folders, photographs, junk food wrappers and paper coffee cups, all surrounding a computer monitor. The contents of the desk were lit by a brass desk lamp with a green glass shade, like something out of an old detective movie, all but a photo frame and a nameplate which remained in shadow. The wire trash bin was filled with crumpled paper balls.

What had caught Ileana's eye was the corkboard behind the desk, wallpapered with pinned photographs, fingerprint cards, newspaper clippings, a map of Los Angeles marked with red circles, documents and mugshots, each connected with red string to a central image. A conspiracy theorist's wet dream, in other words. In the early-2000s Joy had played an alcoholic detective unraveling a plot to tear down the global economy in a direct-to-DVD release universally panned by critics. They'd called it a "crazy wall" during production, and this crazy wall looked eerily similar to what set design had come up with for her office.

Another puzzle that could easily be meant for me.

Joy approached the desk as Atkins moved around it to join Ileana at the corkboard. Only Henry remained by the trapdoor, staring in apparent disbelief at the scene before him.

She spotted Ileana's photo first, a candid shot of her sipping a latté in the driver's seat of a white SUV. She found herself next, a shot of her on the set of *Diamond Dogs*, the heist film she'd done prior to the movie she was currently shooting. Joy remembered the scene they'd been working on that day from her outfit, a tight-fitting black tactical uniform. They'd rigged her up and dropped her into a vault like that scene from the first *Mission Impossible*.

She found Oscar next, and seeing his face again broke her heart. The photo was taken through a window into what looked like a doctor's or dentist's office. He was sitting in a chair in profile, staring straight ahead. Rudy appeared in a museum, looking over a display of African masks. The red strings eventually connected to various papers, photos and clippings to a photo of a familiar building at the center: the Juno Tower in Long Beach.

"It's not all of us," Atkins said. He turned to Henry with an accusatory look. "There's no pictures of Hall on here."

Ileana frowned. "None of you, either. I don't see either of you in any of them."

"I'm not supposed to be here, sister. Remember?"

Joy turned to see Henry was crying. "Are you okay?"

He wiped his eyes with the back of his free hand, the other still holding that terrible Book. "Yeah. Just the gas, I think."

"Bullshit," Atkins said. "He's fucking bawling again."

"Leave him alone."

"*Leave him alone?* I want him to explain why he's not in any of these goddamn pictures."

"There is *one* with him," Ileana said, looking down at the desk. Joy followed her gaze to the framed photo behind the nameplate. From here it was clear to see in the sphere of light from the desk lamp: a photo of a much younger Henry pushing a little girl on a swing.

"What the fuck?" Atkins snatched the nameplate off the desk and turned it to face Henry. "You wanna explain this, Hall?"

Joy read the name engraved in the brass plaque and felt her stomach drop as if she'd just rocketed up ten floors in a runaway elevator.

DET. HENRY HALL, it said.

"This isn't my office," Henry said, his voice fragile as another tear tracked down his cheek. "This is Baskin's. I never..." He shook his head, unable or unwilling to finish.

"Why is there a photo of you and some kid on this desk if

it's not yours?" Ileana said. "Why do you have pictures of all of us and *bank records* and my *fucking college transcripts* on this wall?"

"I *told* you, this isn't my office. It belongs to someone at the same precinct as me, different department. Detective Adam Baskin from Major Crimes."

Ileana crossed her arms. "Oh, sure..."

"Yeah, so why does it have your name and a photo of you and your kid on it, huh?" Atkins grunted. "You been playing us all along? You *following* these people?"

"I told you—"

"Henry," Joy said. "Henry, what's happening?"

"I don't know, Joy. But all of this, everything that's happening here is tied to Infiniti Enterprises." He pointed to the corkboard, to the photo of Juno Tower.

Atkins shook his head. "Conspiracy bullshit."

"Joy, you said yourself Alexei was different after he got involved with Infiniti. Rudy told me he was contacted by someone who claimed to be with them, that they coerced him into discrediting the man who found *this Book*—" He held up the item in question. "—and discontinuing his own search for it."

Atkins squinted at him. "When did he say that?"

"When you all were on the ladder."

Ileana sputtered. "How convenient!"

"Look, I don't know *how* all of this fits into place, but these people are *clearly* trying to play us against each other. It's what they've done—"

He stopped there, his eyes widening.

"What?" Joy asked. "What they've done, what?"

"Since the beginning," he said, pondering something as the hand holding the Book fell to his side.

Joy wasn't sure what she believed about Infiniti, but she knew Henry was telling the truth, or what he *believed* to be the truth. Despite being the only one in a prison uniform, she trusted him more than the other two. Everything she'd seen him do since they'd entered this house was to try and help get them out.

Aside from convincing us to stay in the first place, she thought, though it had been Alexei mentioning Infiniti that convinced her to keep going.

"Whatever's going on here," she said calmly, "we need to figure out how to open that door. Accusing each other of *whatever* isn't helping."

"You're right," Ileana said, having calmed somewhat. She turned back to the board. "Let's look for clues, I guess."

While Atkins tried the desk drawer, Joy stepped around behind it and flicked on the computer monitor. It came on blindingly bright in the semi-dark office. The background was dark blue with LOS ANGELES POLICE DEPARTMENT across the top alongside an LAPD badge. In the lower right corner was a faded image of the current City of L.A. seal: a Tongvan woman standing at the foot of the Pacific, a set of engineering tools, schooner and tuna to her left, the Hollywood Bowl, the San Gabriel Mission and a cow to her right, all symbols meant to represent the area and its history. In the middle of the screen was a square grid of seemingly random numbers.

"What's this?" she asked the others. "Some kind of cipher?"

Atkins shrugged, glancing up from the drawer. "Looks like Suduko."

"It's Su-*doh*-ku, not Suduko," Ileana said, looking back from the board. "But that right there looks like it could be a pattern password. My son has it on his phone. Super easy to crack with finger smudges. His pattern's a sixty-nine, in case you were wondering."

"This one doesn't look like it'll be that easy," Joy said, noticing the pristine layer of dust on the screen. "Looks like no one's touched it in a while."

"It's also got twenty or thirty more numbers," Ileana added.

Atkins sighed. "Great. So, we just have to find whatever correlates to these numbers and figure it out, right? That won't be like looking for a needle in a haystack at all. Hall, get over here and help us find this shit."

Henry wiped his eyes again before crossing the room to them. "We're in a detective's office," he said. "That'll likely be significant to how we solve this puzzle. Let's look for a magnifying glass or a flashlight or a fingerprint brush, something we can use to see things in a different light."

Joy scanned the contents of the desk as Atkins started randomly sifting through them, pushing things aside, knocking over coffee cups—one or two of which had clumps of mold in the bottoms, an authentic touch she hadn't required—and causing a mug to tip over, scattering the pens inside.

"Take it easy, huh?" Henry said, scowling up at him while trying to pry open the filing cabinet. "Messing this place up isn't gonna make this any easier."

"Hey, you look your way, I'll look mine."

Joy regarded the table lamp, thinking about how Henry had phrased his suggestion. *Different light, different light...* She noticed something odd. "There's two bulbs in this lamp," she said. Only one of them was on.

Henry stood and came to her side. He crouched again, squinting at the lamp. "It looks like a blacklight."

Without thinking, Joy reached out and pulled the solid brass switch. The room instantly flooded with purple light, only muted where the light from the computer screen fell. Already she could see areas of bright blue that looked like they might be numbers or letters in several places. She tilted the shade and spotted more on the walls and objects within the room.

"Looks like a strip joint in here," Atkins said, grinning with glowing white teeth.

"Real classy," Ileana shot back, her eyes like a dead fish's.

Joy returned to the computer monitor, planning to turn it off. What she saw stopped her with a hand held out.

The screensaver was something she'd grown familiar with in her years of making action films: a shooting range. The difference was the targets here were pixelated images of herself, Henry and Ileana. A red weapon sight bounced around the screen, skipping menacingly over the three of them at random, at which point each cartoon version of them squeezed their eyes shut. The whole thing looked like something out of an old video game. At the top was another timer, counting down from nine minutes and forty seconds.

She must have triggered it when she flicked the lamp

switch.

"What the fuck is that?" Ileana pointed at the monitor with a sneer, standing just outside its glow.

"It's us," Joy said distractedly, scanning the walls and ceiling for gun holes. She didn't see any but she wasn't naïve enough to believe it made them safe.

Henry peered over Joy's shoulder. "And it looks like we've got nine minutes and thirty seconds to solve this thing before they make us human targets."

"Jesus," Atkins said. "Would it kill them to give us *one* easy one?"

Ileana huffed. "What are you bitching about? You're not on there."

"And guards weren't part of the Attica riot, you think that got them any less dead when the shooting started?"

"Set your watch," Joy told him.

Atkins did, quickly pressing the button until it matched the countdown on the screen. Joy pressed the spacebar. The shooting range vanished and the LAPD background and pattern grid reappeared.

"Let's spread out," she said, taking charge since Henry no longer seemed up to the task. Something about seeing the photo with his daughter, maybe. She wondered how long he'd been away from her. She wondered what a police detective could have done to get him stuck in prison.

You know the answer to that, she thought.

She did, but she didn't want to give credence to any of her assumptions. He *seemed* like a good man. But Ileana had said he was serving fifteen years for premeditated murder. Maybe he'd been set up, and he was actually an innocent man. He could have killed a bad person, a serial killer or human trafficker, to prevent them from taking another victim. It could've been a revenge killing, someone who'd shot his partner or relative or spouse.

Or maybe he just lost it on someone, she thought.

Joy shuddered. After all the deaths they'd witnessed today and how strongly Henry had tried to prevent them, she couldn't let herself believe he was capable of something like that. He'd likely used his service pistol to defend victims of crimes or even himself often. But *murder*... that was a different beast.

Especially *premeditated*.

Atkins, on the other hand. Joy could believe he'd killed someone with malice. It was the eyes—dark and beady like a shark's. He was vicious and mean, and it was clear he didn't give a damn about any of them, only about saving his own ass. Ileana had killed someone to save her own life, but since then she'd attempted to risk her life in the money booth, putting the welfare of the team over her own. Still, Joy wasn't sure she could trust the woman if it came down to the two of them.

Her odds of survival were higher with Henry on her side. Even if this did happen to be an accurate recreation of his office, with their names and faces on his corkboard. Even if it turned out he actually was a convicted murderer.

"There's something circled here," Ileana said, scanning the board. She pointed one out with a long-nailed finger, on a document pinned beneath her own photo, then moved closer to inspect it, squinting in the semi-dark. "'Lo, the mouth of a great beast stretched across the firmament,'" she read. "What the fuck does that mean?"

"Sounds like something out of the Book of Revelation," Henry said, deep in thought. His eyes lit up and he laid the Book down on the table in front of the lamp, opening it to the first page.

"What are you doing?" Joy asked.

He looked up at her, his face alien in the purple light. "Remember when we thought the images might be made with invisible ink?"

She nodded.

"Look," he said, pointing at the page.

Joy looked closer. The fourth and fifth pages had filled in with an image of an emaciated woman sweeping a hand across a landscape of dead foliage and dying people under a black sky. Clearly this was meant to be Achlys, goddess of poison and eternal night. Printed within the black sky, tiny words glowed. A sentence, but unreadable due to its size. "It's words."

"We need a magnifying glass."

120

"There's a number beside the quote," Ileana said. "Five-one-three."

Henry picked up a piece of paper and pen. He scratched on the paper with the pen to make sure it worked, then wrote: *5 1 3 Lo, the mouth of a great beast stretched across…*

"Across the what, Ileana?"

"The firmament," she repeated.

"Anyone know what a firmament is?" Henry asked as he wrote it on the paper.

"I think it means sky or the heavens," Joy said as she returned to the monitor, sure she must have learned it in Sunday school. There were lots of fives, ones and threes in the grid but she couldn't easily see any together, nor how they might work together as a passcode. As she looked, she noticed some of the numbers appeared to be double digits. She spotted at least five fifty-ones and seven or eight thirteens. There were far too many repeated numbers to solve the code without knowing what to look for.

"There's a keyhole in this drawer," Atkins said beside her.

Henry left the Book and slipped between Joy and Ileana to Atkins's side. Joy saw him study the keyhole a moment and reach behind himself, fingers touching his back pocket before he visibly decided against it. "I could jimmy this lock if we had a couple of paperclips," he said.

Joy scanned the desk for one, or anything that could be used in lieu of it. Atkins once again pushed great swaths of items aside with the only apparent motive of making an even bigger mess. Fortunately, he happened to uncover a small leather pouch in his aimlessness. Joy snatched it up before he could bury it again and unzipped it.

"What is that?" Ileana asked.

Joy opened the pouch, allowing a smile to reach her lips for the first time she could remember today as she looked at its contents. "I'll do you one better," she said, holding it open for the others to see.

Henry laughed. He took the lockpick kit from her and slipped out two small tools. Then he dropped to a crouch and began working away at the lock.

121

"Where'd you learn how to do that, Hall? Juvie?"

"Funny," Henry said, fiddling with the tools. A moment later a tiny click came from the lock and the drawer popped open.

"I'll take those," Atkins said, holding out a hand for the picks.

Reluctantly, Henry handed them over.

"You too, sister," Atkins said, turning to Joy.

"I'll keep these safe," she said, zipping up the pouch and slipping it into her back pocket.

Atkins gave her a hard look, then tucked the errant tools into the pocket on his lapel with a sneer.

Henry pulled the drawer open the rest of the way. "It's our lucky day."

Ileana sputtered. "I wouldn't go that far."

Henry reached into the drawer and came up holding a magnifying glass, which he held up to his nose, making his already alien eye look stranger.

He returned to the Book. Joy joined him. Placing the magnifying glass over the glowing words, he read them aloud as he moved it along the page. "'Five-one-eight, Pestilence and Famine rode upon their backs.'" Jotting the numbers and phrase on the page, he added, "Sounds like the Four Horsemen of the Apocalypse."

Joy looked at the two sentences together, along with their corresponding numbers. "Five-one again. Maybe it's *fifty-one* eight. Like a Bible quote."

"So, we're looking for numbers beside fifty-one," Henry said. "That narrows it down."

"Seven minutes," Atkins said, looking at the screen rather than his watch. The screensaver had returned, the target sight dancing faster across the screen.

Joy pressed the spacebar, causing the number grid to return. She found the eight beside a fifty-one relatively easily. It took her longer to find fifty-one three because the three was below it, rather than beside it.

"Is it safe to assume we're looking for consecutive numbers?" she asked.

Henry shrugged. "I guess it can't hurt to try..."

"How do you know it won't speed up the countdown?" Atkins said, frowning down at Henry in the glow of the monitor.

"Nothing we've done has messed with the timer before. I say it's worth a try."

Joy agreed with a nod. She searched the grid for a two near a fifty-one. She found it at the top, right in the middle, and considered it a good sign.

"There's a quote on the first page," Henry said, sliding the magnifying glass across the top. "'The sun disappeared from the sky, and the Heavens rained with blood.'"

"Any numbers?"

"Fifty-one one and fifty-one two," he said, jotting them down on the page.

"There's another quote here," Ileana said. It was partly out of the glow of the UV light. She took the pin out of the board, letting it dangle on the red string, and brought the loose page over to the lamp to inspect it. It looked like a California driver's exam. "'One of the earliest known symbols of the occult,'" she read from it slowly, "'the first... this word is smudged... was discovered in Sumer on clay pottery found in the city of Ur.'"

Joy found fifty-one four on the pattern lock, three numbers up from the bottom on the right side.

Henry jotted the phrase down in bullet points. "No numbers?"

"Not that I can see."

"Okay." He flipped the page and drew the magnifying glass across the top of the pages showing Marbas, the lion-faced giant, leading his legions of demons across a fiery landscape. "'Lo, the mouth... of the Watcher... stretched wide across the firmament... and from the Great Beast's jaws ... came Legion,'" he read, then returned to the page to jot it down.

"'The Watcher,'" Ileana repeated, hugging herself with a dramatic shiver. "Totally not creepy at all."

Joy began to draw out the path in her mind while Henry tapped the end of the pen on the page like a drumstick. "Aha!" he cried, just as Joy said, "Wait!" She found a three under a fifty-one on the left side, the same distance from the top as fifty-one four, and mentally traced the path between the numbers. "It's a pentagram!"

"That's what I was thinking," Henry said.

Atkins got between them, holding out a hand. "Wait, wait—you guys are sure about this?"

Henry nodded at the screen. "Rudy said that Marbas commands thirty-six legions of demons, remember? He said Marbas is the Great President of Hell. One of the oldest symbols is the pentagram, it's also a Satanic symbol. It makes sense."

Joy agreed. She spotted the next numbers on the top at about the same distance from the left side as the right. The odds were pretty high.

"We all need to agree on this," Henry said, staring Atkins down.

Ileana nodded. "It sounds right."

Atkins grunted. "Fine. Do it."

Joy touched the space between fifty-one and one and traced a diagonal line up to fifty-one two. Her finger cut through the dust but also created a visible red line on the screen. She dragged it diagonally to three, straight across to four, up to five and back down to one. Then the number grid vanished, leaving only the inverted red pentagram.

The screen unlocked.

Six folders were bunched closely together in the center, each under one of their names, all but Henry's and Atkins's. Even Jessica Danvers had a folder. Joy moved the mouse over to her own folder and clicked twice. It was empty. She clicked on Ileana's and found nothing in that one, either.

"What's that?" Henry said with a look of deep concern furrowing his brow. He reached past her, pointing out a folder all by itself near the upper right corner of the screen. It was labeled "NUNGAL."

"Maybe one of the previous players?" she said.

"I don't think so. Open it."

Joy double-clicked on the folder. It was password protected with five digits.

"Jesus," Atkins said. "Give us a fucking break."

"Five numbers," Joy said.

"Or letters," Henry added. "Try our first initials."

"In what order?"

Henry reached over her hands for the keyboard.

"Excuse me, Mr. Man," Ileana said.

"It's fine," Joy told her, stepping back as Henry began typing. His fingers moved swiftly but she saw he'd started with J—making a reasonable assumption that the code would begin with the name of the codemaker's spouse—then O for Oscar, then H for himself, then R and I, leaving out only the second J for the woman they'd never met. Nothing. He tried again, starting with J and a different combination.

"Six minutes," Atkins said, eyeing his watch.

Ileana hummed. "Out of curiosity, how many password combinations can you make from five letters?"

"Too many," Joy said. "There has to be something with our names on the board."

Henry nodded. "Check the board. I'll keep running through combinations."

Joy and Ileana returned to study the board. Atkins appeared content to keep watching Henry.

Joy looked at her photograph. She'd been caught in an unflattering expression, sort of a half grimace half smile. Directly above her photo, attached by red string, was a non-disclosure agreement she'd signed early in her career. Just looking at it, understanding that Alexei must have shared it with his friends at Infiniti, made her skin crawl. She wanted to tear it off the board and rip it to shreds, but doing so would draw attention to it. It would cause more trouble than leaving it be.

Behind her, Henry's fingers rattled over the keys, his chains jingling like wind chimes. She forced herself to ignore the NDA and focus on the board as a whole. There were likely incriminating things about all of them on here. She wondered what Ileana was hiding out in the open. She seemed like the kind of woman with a shady past she'd desperately tried to leave behind.

She spotted another quote Ileana had missed, written in the

blue-white glowing text over an admission letter to the Olympia University for Trent Foxworth, Alexei's attorney. It was signed by Jessica Danvers, Dean of Admissions. The phrase scrawled over it was: ...*and the disbelievers were washed away in the Flood.*

Reading it sent a shiver up her spine.

Joy let her eyes unfocus, staring at the board as if it was a magic eye painting. The red string reminded her of something she'd just seen. She stepped back, then held out a hand to cover Jessica Danvers' photo from her sight. It clicked immediately. "Without Jessica Danvers, our photos make a pentagram," she said.

"Five letters," Henry said. "Shit, why didn't I think of that? What's the order?"

Joy tried to remember the order in which she'd drawn the inverted pentagram. "Try... J-O-I-H-R."

She remained looking at the board while Henry typed out five strokes.

"It opened," Henry said behind her.

She and Ileana joined him at the computer.

"Five minutes," Atkins said.

The folder had five PDF documents, one for each of the captives who'd made it beyond the entry rooms.

"Open mine," Ileana said, crowding in beside Atkins, her eager face bathed in the bluish glow of the screen.

Henry did.

The document was a grainy photocopy of a Superior Court of Iowa arrest warrant.

"What the fuck?" Ileana said, stepping back in apparent shock. She looked at the others. Her eyes locked with Joy's for a moment, then quickly returned to the screen. She snatched at the mouse in Henry's hand. He jerked it away before she could grab it.

Joy immediately spotted her reason for freaking out. The defendant listed on the warrant was Ileana Doukas. The charges were INVOLUNTARY MANSLAUGHTER and RECKLESS HOMICIDE. Joy figured she must've changed her name from Doukas to Athanasiou either in marriage or to hide these charges.

"Ho-lee shit," Atkins said, letting out a surprised laugh.

"That's not any of your business!" Ileana shouted, attempting to cover the image with her hands before giving up and flicking off the screen.

"If there's stuff in there about the rest of us, I wanna know," Henry said.

Ileana gave him a vicious glare. "As if there'd be stuff about *you*."

"We don't have time for that," Joy said, hoping to diffuse the situation. "We need to figure out how to open that door and get the hell out of here."

Atkins nodded. "She's right. It doesn't matter whether the Honorable Senator Athanasiou killed someone in cold blood or not."

"It was an accident!" Ileana cried, tears streaming down her face. "It was just hazing! Everybody had to go through it to get into Omega Alpha! We were just stupid kids, that's all. It was… it was just an accident."

Nobody said anything.

Ileana's eyes went wide. She looked down and grabbed at Atkins's side. The gun came free of its holster and she regarded it briefly held in both hands, seemingly stunned she'd been able to grab it so easily. Atkins reached out and she pointed it at him. The gun clattered in her jittery hands.

"Get back!"

Everyone took a step back, including Ileana herself.

"Just relax, sister."

"Don't you fucking 'sister' me! *Why do you have this?*" she demanded, pointing the gun shakily toward Henry. "*Why are you doing this to us?*"

Henry threw up his hands.

"It's not him," Joy said.

"How do you know that, huh? It's his nameplate on the desk. It's his picture with his daughter. Do you know what he did to land in prison?"

"Ileana…" Henry said.

"*Shut up!* A woman is speaking, so you shut up and listen.

127

I'll tell you what he did. His little girl—" She pointed to the framed photograph on the desk. "—his innocent little girl was raped and murdered by a fucking detective in his own precinct. And when he found out, he went to that man's house in the middle of the night, and he shot him point blank in the head. He messed things around and stole a few things to make it look like a home invasion. That man's name was Adam Baskin."

"This is *his* office," Henry said again.

"*I don't believe you!*" she spat.

"Come on," Atkins said calmly. "Put down the gun."

"He's not leaving this room! This is the end of the line, Henry Hall. Right here."

"Ileana, listen to yourself," Joy said. "This is crazy."

"Is it? He said it himself, one of us has to die in each of these rooms. These are *rituals*. You want that door to open, one of us has to spill fucking blood, and it's not gonna be me, I'll tell you that! It happened to Jessica Danvers, it happened to Oscar and Rudy... So why not him next? Huh? Who's gonna miss one more murdering scumbag rotting away behind bars, wasting tax dollars?"

"*There* she is," Atkins said with a sly grin. "There's that 'tough on crime' District Attorney I remember."

Ileana turned to him with the gun still held on Henry. In a quick move Henry reached into his back pocket and came up with something shiny and metallic. Had he palmed one of the lockpicks? Whatever it was, he stepped forward and slashed it across Ileana's forearm as she turned to face him. The gun went off, as loud as a cannon. Joy held her ears but it made the ringing worse. Ileana startled and leaped back a step, but Henry followed her. He grabbed her arm, pushed it upwards, then twisted it and snatched the gun from her hand. It wasn't quite as elegant as the Krav Maga techniques Joy had learned for the first *Arrowheart* film, but it did the trick.

Ileana screamed, squeezing her eyes shut and thrusting her hands up in the air. Blood dripped down her right forearm to the floor and she dropped to a crouch in the corner of the room. "Don't kill me—*please don't kill me!*"

"I'm not gonna hurt you, Ileana, for Christ's sake!" he said, tucking the metallic object back in his pocket.

Joy saw Atkins take a single step forward. She called Henry's name. Henry whipped around, raising the gun. Atkins stopped in his tracks and shot a look back at her.

"You dumb bitch."

Henry held out his hands. "Take these chains off."

"We've got four fucking minutes here, Hall. What are you planning to do? Fucking yoga?"

"Just shut up and take them off, goddammit!"

Shaking his head, Atkins said, "Fine. Goddamn waste of time, you ask me." He stepped forward, then stopped. "You're not gonna fucking shoot me, are you?"

"Don't make any stupid decisions and I won't have to."

"Stupid decisions." Atkins sputtered. "This whole day's been *full* of 'em. Hell, it's been stupid decisions ever since I took this fucking job."

"Joy?" Henry said. "Take the gun?"

Joy held his gaze a moment, surprised he trusted her enough to help him. She nodded, and held out a hand.

Atkins sneered back at her. "Well, aren't we just thick as thieves?"

Joy took the gun and pointed it at him, the way she'd been taught in countless tactical gun training lessons. "We don't have time to argue. Just do as he says."

"What makes you think I won't take that thing back from you?"

Joy tilted it to the side, glancing to make sure the safety was off. It was a Glock 22, a .40-caliber pistol standard for the California Department of Corrections, and a weapon she was very familiar with. Not as much stopping power as the .36, but good enough to take him down.

"You could try," she said. "But if you think I won't shoot you twice in the chest before you can say 'Jesus' one last time, you're wrong."

Atkins's sneer widened to a grin. "I knew I liked you for a reason. All right, Hall," he said, still holding Joy's gaze. "Today's your lucky day." He turned his back to her, pulling at the lanyard holding his keys, and unlocked the shackles at

Henry's wrists. They fell to the floor with a jangle and clang. Atkins shook his head and made to crouch, then stopped and gave Henry a hard look. "If you make one fucking move," he warned.

"Just take them off."

Atkins shook his head, then crouched to take off the leg shackles. Henry kicked them aside as Atkins stood.

"All right, you happy, you clowns? Now gimme back my gun."

"Give it to me, Joy," Henry said.

"Bull*shit*, Hall," Atkins snapped.

Henry gave her a pleading look. "Joy. Please."

Joy handed Henry the weapon. He turned it quickly, pointing it at Atkins before the man could attempt to snatch it back. Then he bent, scooped up the chains and shackles, and stepped around to the front of the desk. He crossed to the trapdoor, dropped the shackles on the floor beside it, then wrenched it open. A thick miasma of gas rose from the opening.

"What the fuck are you doing, Hall?"

Henry dropped the chains into the opening. Then he made to do the same with the Glock.

"*Wait wait wait*—"

The chains clattered on the floor far below. Henry's grip relaxed and the Glock dropped in with them. He closed the trapdoor swiftly, the gas cloud eddying up and dissipating in the current of air.

"What the fuck did you do that for, Hall? We could've needed that!"

"You just saw for yourself firsthand," Henry said, returning to the desk. "In a situation like this, none of us can be trusted with a gun."

"How many situations like this have you been in, huh? There *is* no situation like this! We've got—" He glanced at his watch. "—three fucking minutes to figure out how to get out of this fucking room, or we've all just smoked our last fucking cigarettes."

Henry cocked his head in confusion. "Oh, because of the firing squad. That's a good one, Atkins."

"Thanks," the man grunted. "So now fucking what?"

"Now?" Henry turned to face the wall to his left. "Joy, can you point the light this way?"

Joy reached for the light. The shade was hot but she managed to tilt it so that Henry and the wall behind him were bathed in its purple glow. She saw something written in large letters, glowing blue-white but smeared and dripping as if it had been painted in blood—or some other bodily fluid she didn't want to speculate on. It was a very familiar three-word phrase, though it was only the second time she'd ever seen the name.

NUNGAL WAS HERE, it said. A thick, streaky arrow pointed down to a hole in the wall the size of a fist.

"Now, you're getting the hell out of here," Henry said. He crouched and stuck his left hand into the hole, reaching until his elbow touched the wall. There was a sharp *click!* and a *clunk* from the door as the lock disengaged. A strange sound arose the second the door came open, like some kind of haunting music.

Ileana became animated for the first time since Henry took the gun from her. She leaped to her feet with her wide, wet eyes opened in shock. Her forearm was crusted with blood. "How did you—?"

"That name," Joy said. "It was on the folder."

Henry nodded. "Let's get moving. I'll explain when I can."

Nobody needed an engraved invitation. Joy, Atkins, and Ileana hurried around the desk and met Henry at the door. He drew it open, revealing a long, dark hallway lit only by dim overhead hanging lamps which swung to the sound of the— chanting? Humming? Joy couldn't tell. She smelled cold, damp stone and the stench of human waste, both urine and shit, a high, impenetrable stink. The moaned chorus arose from dark, barred cells running along either side. At the far end, an antique cage-style elevator car awaited with the gate open, the brightest spot in the corridor. The hand on the brass dial above moved almost imperceptibly between the second and first floors.

Less than two minutes, she thought.

"*Run*," Henry said, ushering them forward.

Joy stepped into the hallway first. The haunting moans rose in a crescendo. She watched as ghouls in ragged black cloaks rose from the first cells, bare floors and walls made of cold wet stone with no beds and no toilets, just filthy holes in the floor.

She had scant seconds to marvel at how these ancient-looking cells could possibly have gotten here, to a house she'd lived in off and on less than a year ago, when the wretched prisoners rushed the bars. Below their hoods the flesh on their faces was sallow and gray, pulled taut over bone. Their teeth were rotted, tongues shriveled and ululating, as if somewhere within their chorus of plaintive moans were words she couldn't decipher. Horrible sunken eyes burned with a crimson intensity, boring into her. She thought it must be an optical illusion, or an aftereffect of the UV light in the office. The pitiful creatures reached through the bars, scrabbling fingers blackened with dirt and blood, their moans wavering, rising in a fervor.

The passage between their grabbing hands was just wide enough to walk down sideways. She moved quickly but cautiously, forcing herself not to stray in her path when the ragged nails happened to catch her, scratching flesh.

Atkins came next, sneering into the cells before him, rearing back as the hands snatched at his face and shoulders. Fingers caught the nape of his neck and slashed. Whipping around, Atkins got caught again from behind, a ragged man grasping his shirt collar. He managed to shake the fingers free, but caught another slash on his forearm.

"Woulda been better off taking my chances with the gas!" he shouted over their mournful song.

Joy looked beyond him to see Ileana hesitating at the door. The senator looked traumatized, staring in pure terror at the gray-fleshed hands and emaciated arms reaching through the bars from grimy, tattered black cloaks. Henry spoke to her encouragingly, impossible for Joy to hear. He held out a hand to her. She took it warily and he stepped into the room, leading her along.

Resuming her trek, Joy saw the man in front of her had no nose. She regarded it in horror, the flesh surrounding the two holes in his face rotted, his gaping mouth toothless, a raw stub of a tongue wriggling at the back of his throat. His blind, cataract eyes gazed in her direction like those of a dead fish. Was it leprosy? Was he contagious? Joy didn't know, but it was clear from the stench of filth in the cells these men had been here for a long time, possibly ages.

Left in a room with only a bottle of water for six hours, she thought, remembering what she'd told the others, not for sympathy but to offer them a limited understanding of her estranged husband's mental state. Already that moment felt like ages ago, like a scene from an entirely different life. Oscar and Rudy had still been with them. There'd still been a slim hope of escape.

"Move it, sister!" Atkins said, mere feet from her.

Joy broke free from her trance. Had she stopped moving? Something about these pitiable creatures and their atonal song made her lose focus. She was in danger, yet had stood here long enough for Atkins to close the ten-foot gap between them.

She turned away from the man without a nose and resumed her sideways momentum, trying not to look at any of them long enough to lose herself again.

The four of them headed for the elevator, dodging the gnawed fingers as best they could.

Then Ileana screamed.

Henry called out, "*No!*" His voice was barely audibly over the chanting.

Ileana was pinned to the bars, grubby fingers roaming her body, pulling at her dress. Henry reached out then stepped back as a hand shot out, swiping at his face. He hesitated.

"We have to help her!" Joy shouted.

"If we still had the fucking gun we could do something about this, Hall!"

Henry looked back at them. The creatures had pulled up Ileana's dress, scoring her bare legs with ragged claw marks. She screamed again, but a hand shot out and covered her mouth. The horror in her eyes was unlike anything Joy had ever

133

witnessed. She couldn't imagine how awful the hand covering her nose and mouth must have smelled, let alone the terror Ileana was feeling as the hands tore at her chest and arms and legs, pulling her hair.

Henry glanced at the clock. "Go!" he shouted, waving them on.

Reluctantly, Joy kept moving. Atkins followed, his jaw clenched, blood dripping into his left eye from a slash across his forehead.

It seemed like the corridor narrowed as they reached the elevator. Whether it was true or not, skeletal claws on either side managed to grab her arms. She wrestled free and leaped into the elevator, turning around just as Atkins jumped in behind her.

"Jesus fucking Christ!" he gasped, breathing heavily.

Joy could barely catch her own breath, and what she saw when she peered down the passage of writhing flesh made it catch in her throat. Henry fought against the sea of grabbing hands, but Ileana was already gone, her throat slashed, her head tilted upward, staring at the swinging light hung above her. Hands tore her dress, exposing her breasts and stomach. They tore into her flesh, digging into her abdomen, pulling out bloody ropes of intestines and slimy organs, feasting on her innards like horror film zombies.

Henry turned away with a look of despair and ran for the elevator, his upper body twisted enough that the hands reached him but running at a fast enough pace they weren't able to catch hold.

Ileana's body had fallen to the floor. Hands fought over gore-soaked scraps of flesh and clothing. She was a human buffet, her lifeblood spreading out in a pool around her.

Henry burst through the elevator door with the Book tucked under an arm, his face covered with blood, some his own, most of it Ileana's. He turned quickly and pulled the gate shut. "Get us out of here," he cried, unable to take his eyes off the atrocity in the hall.

Joy glanced at the control panel. Only one button was intact, in the bottom right corner, none of them numbered. She pressed it.

The elevator jostled, startling them all. They gave each other a brief look of shared commiseration and fear and something none of them could articulate. But the message was clear: there'd been nothing they could do.

The elevator descended.

"Next floor: Hell," Atkins grunted sarcastically.

Astoundingly, Henry began to laugh.

THE FACTS

NEXT FLOOR: HELL," Atkins said as the elevator began its rickety descent. Henry turned to watch the corridor of horrors slip out of sight, taking one last look at Ileana's shredded remains. He hadn't liked her, had considered her rude, selfish and self-absorbed, but she hadn't deserved such a grisly death. None of them had.

As the cells and their wretched prisoners disappeared, and the droning of that horrible chorus diminished, Henry surprised himself by laughing, and once he'd gotten started he found he couldn't stop. He laughed until his skull ached and his ribcage felt bruised. He laughed even as Joy and Atkins gave him concerned looks, worried for his sanity. And honestly, he worried for it himself. This morning he'd been sitting in his cell, contemplating another thirteen years alone with his guilt and sorrow, staring at his painting of Clara which kept hidden the words he'd just found written in blood or piss or shit washed off the wall in the office of his daughter's murderer. Either he'd lost his mind, or this was a terrible, endless nightmare from which he couldn't seem to wake.

Or we really are in Hell…

Thinking this, his laughter abruptly stopped.

"What are we gonna do now?" Joy asked in the sudden silence, tears and blood streaking her face. "We can't keep doing this." She turned to him first, then Atkins. "Can we?"

"Doing what?"

"Playing his game. Completing these rituals."

"What choice do we have?" Atkins said. He folded his arms

across his chest, leaned back against the wall and sank to the floor. "We just keep playing until we get out of this fucking place." He looked up at Henry, blinking blood from his left eye. "Right? I mean what fucking choice do we have, huh?"

Joy shook her head and sank into the other corner, hugging her knees. Henry joined them, leaning against the wall under the control box as the elevator car sank down and down toward God knew what.

Maybe God doesn't even know, he thought.

"Those things…" Joy said. "I don't think they were human."

Atkins sputtered. "They were human, all right."

"They ate… they ate Ileana…"

"You'd be surprised what people would do to—" He stopped there, likely realizing he'd said this before, that they were beyond surprise at this point. "They'd probably been starved for who knows how long. Hell, I'm pretty sure they were eating each other. You see that one ugly fuck with no nose?"

Joy shuddered.

"They were chanting something," Henry said. "I heard words. When they… when Ileana died. 'Glory,' they said. 'Glory to her. Glory to Nungal.'"

"I heard it, too," Joy said, rocking forward and back now, still hugging her knees. "But who *is* Nungal?"

"Nungal is a Mesopotamian goddess. The ruler of the underworld. Protector of prisoners."

Atkins chortled. "You sound like Rudy."

"The reason I know is because that same phrase we saw back there, with the arrow pointing to that hole where the lever was, it's scratched into the wall in my cell."

Joy's eyes widened. "*What?*"

"You gotta be kidding, Hall."

"The same words I keep covered with a painting I did of my… my sweet Clarabelle…" His throat locked. Tears threatened again, as they had back in the office while he stared in disbelief at the desk of her murderer, somehow bearing his own nameplate and the photo Mercy had taken of him pushing Clara on the swing that day in Griffith Park. He'd managed to compose himself, but the tears had still come, and Joy had noticed. Atkins, too. Joy seemed to watch over him with some protective instinct, the way she'd acted toward Oscar. For some reason, she seemed to trust him. Atkins merely watched him like a hound. Or like a vulture waiting for him to die.

As he thought this, Rudy's final words echoed in his mind: *I believe your ward is working against us.*

"Clara is your daughter?" Joy asked cautiously.

"Was. She was my daughter. She's gone now. The man whose office that was…" He couldn't go on, not that it mattered. Ileana had already told them. But she hadn't known how it felt knowing one of his own had done a thing so unspeakable to a member of his family. She hadn't known how *betrayed* Henry had felt, not just grief-stricken. Detective Adam Baskin had raped the teenage daughter of one of his brothers and sisters in blue, and murdered her in an attempt to cover up his actions when he'd discovered she was one of his own.

When that lawyer showed up at Henry's door with a signed confession, he hadn't known *what* to think. He'd assumed Clara's death had been the act of some sick junkie or desperate street kid carjacker. The truth was, Baskin had pulled her over. It was her first night driving alone. She'd told Henry and her mom she was going to a friend's house to "study," though Henry was pretty certain she'd been headed to a party. Baskin had seen a lone girl in a car and pulled her over under the pretense that she'd been speeding. He'd used his badge to scare her into submission and forced himself on her, like something out of those sick pornos, some sadistic power trip.

He'd been smart. He'd used a condom, even though it went against his "every instinct as a man," in his words. But when he'd gone looking through her purse he'd seen a photo of her with Henry. Middle school graduation, Henry figured. Baskin had lost it, realizing what he'd just done couldn't be walked back. So, while Clara wept in the backseat, Baskin grabbed the tire iron which was under the front seat from when Mercy had popped a tire a few weeks prior. He'd swung it at her head again and again until her face was nothing but a mashed pulp of flesh and bone tangled in her auburn curls. He'd wiped down everything he might have touched before he'd put his gloves on and left the car. He'd smashed in the driver's window and sprinkled a handful of broken glass over Clara's mangled head. Then he'd driven off to meet back up with the boys at the tavern some of them frequented, to solidify his alibi should he require one.

Henry had read the confession repeatedly until his eyes misted with tears and his hands shook, trying to fathom what could have driven a man of the law to do such terrible things. The lawyer—something Foxworth, Henry thought his name was, Brent or Kent—had told him that Baskin had signed the confession as a plea deal. He expected the man to serve a maximum of ten years. A single dime in a cushy cell in protective custody for raping and murdering Clara.

Henry found his shaking fingers could no longer hold on to the confession. It had fallen to the floor between them. The lawyer made no move to pick it up.

"I'm telling you this, Henry." He'd taken him by the shoulders and forced him to look up. "I'm telling you this because there's still a chance for you to do something about it. Ten years is no kind of punishment. Not for something like this. I'm telling you this because I know you'll know what to do with this information. Am I correct in that assumption, Henry?"

Henry had blinked away his tears. He'd sniffled and wiped his nose on his sleeve. Then he'd nodded.

"Just so there's no future misunderstanding," Foxworth had said. He held out a second document. "If you could sign this, please."

"W-what is it?"

"Just a standard non-disclosure agreement, stating that you and I never had this meeting." He handed Henry a gold pen. Henry regarded it a moment, then took both the pen and NDA. Foxworth turned his back, intending Henry to sign the document on it. Henry looked it over, but his mind was elsewhere. It could have been written in Mandarin for all he knew. He didn't think about how signing this could affect him in the future. He only knew for certain what he planned to do with the information he'd been provided.

It was one of the easiest things in the world, killing a man.

Getting away with it was the difficult part.

What Ileana had said was true. Henry had killed Baskin in cold blood and, just as Baskin had with Clara's murder, attempted to cover it up with a robbery. He'd been thorough and meticulous, making sure to leave no fingerprints, then smashed lamps and overturned furniture and yanked open drawers, pouring out their contents, making it look like a smash and grab, a home invasion gone wrong. He'd even thrown the gun he'd used, an untraceable Glock .9mm he'd stolen from the evidence locker when he'd gone in to check some items from a factory fire in the L.A. River.

Yet somehow that gun was discovered within days of the murder. Worse, prosecutors had footage of him stealing it, even though he'd done it out of sight of the security cameras. They'd placed hidden cameras, was the official explanation, because they suspected someone was stealing large quantities of fentanyl and selling it on the street.

Discovering this after the fact, once he'd already been arrested and charged with murder, made him start to pull at the threads. How, for instance, had they gotten Baskin's confession so easily, wrapped up in a nice bow like it was? That was something he pondered day after day in his lonely cell as the trial stretched on. Foxworth could easily have been Baskin's lawyer, but what sort of defense attorney would sell out his client like that? What would he have stood to gain?

After that day at his front door, Henry had expected never to see the lawyer again. But Brent or Kent Foxworth had been there in the courtroom while the jury read their verdict. He'd grinned as the judge handed down a sentence of fifteen years.

Everything made sense now. It had been a setup, right from the very beginning. Baskin hadn't raped and murdered Clara or possibly anyone. Infiniti had framed him, because he'd been on to them. They'd paid someone to molest and murder his daughter knowing he would seek vengeance on the man they'd pinned it on. They got rid of Baskin and his investigation, and had a patsy to take the fall, just like they had with the fire in Long Beach.

All of the pieces had fallen into place the moment he saw

the corkboard in the recreation of Baskin's office, like a puzzle without a box. It all pointed directly to Infiniti. Henry had gone into Baskin's office the morning before he'd killed the man, just to try and understand him a little, to get into his psyche. The board had looked exactly the same, down to each key player. He hadn't retained much information, but he remembered every one of their faces: Rudy, Oscar, Joy, Ileana and Jessica. It was the photos of the apartment fire, connected to the picture of Oscar with red string, that had drawn his attention. Between them and the center of the pegboard was a snapshot of the Apollo Pharmaceuticals building along with several newspaper clippings of "freak" viral outbreaks, declaring Oscar a hero. They'd all tied back to a blank space in the middle which had clearly once been occupied by the photo of Infiniti's headquarters, just as it had in the office puzzle.

He'd murdered a man for nothing. Not just any man, either: a fellow police officer, someone whose only crime was looking a little too deeply in the wrong direction. A direction leading to Infiniti Enterprises, and ultimately, to this fucking house.

"What wasn't him?" Joy asked, drawing him from his thoughts.

"Huh?" Henry hadn't realized he'd spoken aloud, but he'd clearly said something. No use trying to walk it back now. "Detective Baskin. He didn't kill my Clara. It was Infiniti."

"Why would Infiniti kill your daughter?"

"To frame him. He was getting too close. Investigating them. That corkboard in there—"

"The crazy wall," she said.

"—that's Baskin's work. He was close to them. He had theories, I guess. I remember some of the guys saying he was losing it. Getting squirrely. But he was right. It all ties back to Infiniti. *We* all do. Every one of us."

"Except me," Atkins reminded him. "I'm not supposed to be here, remember?"

Henry ignored the man. "Infiniti has their fingers in every facet of this city. Government, disease control, education, history, infrastructure, entertainment, probably the police department. It could even go well beyond L.A."

"They have members from all over the world," Joy said. "Superyacht people—involved with Davos and Bilderberg, probably Skull and Bones and the Illuminati, too, for all I know."

"Next thing you'll tell me is they're affiliated with the grey aliens," Atkins quipped. "Yeah, they're helping them take over the planet, huh?"

"Nothing would surprise me at this point," she said. "I told you, Alexei *changed* after he got involved with them. And those men they've got held prisoner up there? That shit was *beyond* abnormal."

"I don't think they were prisoners," Henry said. "I think they're cultists. 'Glory to Nungal.' They don't teach us that tune behind bars."

Atkins chuckled.

"Why would the same phrase in your prison cell be written on the wall back there?" Joy asked.

"Obviously somebody meant to give us a hint. Whether or not that's a *good* thing is up for grabs. To be honest, I wasn't sure when I stuck my hand in there whether it was the way out or just another trap."

"Someone on the inside," Atkins remarked. "Huh."

"I'd be willing to bet whoever scratched it into the wall in my cell knew where they'd be holding me. Meaning: this plan has been a long time in the making. I wasn't picked at random, and neither were you and the others, Joy."

"Well, what was that stuff in the Book about the 'great mouth'? That sounds like prophecy to me."

With all the horror they'd just experienced, Henry had forgotten about the Book. It lay on the floor beside him, Ileana's blood drying in streaks on its pale leather face.

He picked it up and opened it, flipping past the art and script in ancient languages for the demons Apep and Marbas and the goddess Achlys, to the pages for Nungal containing new images and what was likely Mesopotamian cuneiform. The crowned and robed goddess stood on a hill with a large dog beside her, overlooking a sea of people in yokes and chains, most of whom were prostrate before her. Fearsome-looking winged creatures circled the stormy firmament, occasionally descending upon the prisoners.

Henry turned the Book to face the others. Joy leaned closer over her knees. Atkins glanced at it, then turned away as if it might burn his retinas.

"I wish Rudy was here to translate all this stuff."

Joy crawled across the elevator floor to join him. "Can I see?"

He held it out to her. She shook her head with a fearful look.

"I don't want to hold it. I don't want to *touch* it."

Henry couldn't say he blamed her. He held it up for her to look at in detail.

"So that's supposed to be Nungal?"

"I guess so."

"And the dog?"

"I couldn't really find much about the dog. Some sites called it Bau, but then others called Bau a goddess, and others said she was the daughter of some Sumerian king. I guess there's a lot of conflicting information about some of the gods and goddesses from back then."

Atkins chortled.

"Anyway, some websites used the name Gula for Bau. When I was looking *that* up, a fortunate typo made me stumble on the *gallu*."

"What's that?" Joy said, looking up at him with wide, red-rimmed eyes.

"These things, I think," Henry said, pointing out the flying creatures in the darksome sky. "They're demons. Ancient Sumerians believed the gallu kidnapped people and brought them to the underworld."

"I guess we didn't need Rudy after all," Atkins muttered.

Henry ignored him. "If these really are all rituals, then we've already performed three of them."

"Four," Atkins said. "Remember? The chick with the snakes?"

"Right, four. I don't know how many more rooms we'll have to get through to get out of this place, but I have a bad feeling these people never intended us to. There's only four more pages in this Book."

Joy's eyes widened as she understood the point. "Two more rituals," she said. "Two more deaths."

"Right. That said, I doubt people this meticulous would be content to leave loose ends."

Joy followed his gaze to Atkins, who was picking something wet off his boot with a sneer. He looked up at them.

"What? What did I do?" Before either of them could reply, the elevator shook and grumbled. Atkins looked up with unmasked fear. "What the hell was that?"

Joy stood, looking at the walls passing by with growing concern. "How fucking far down does this elevator shaft go?"

Henry looked up, through the caged roof of the elevator car. The corridor they'd left was nothing more than a pinprick of light seemingly hundreds of feet above them.

"Maybe it *is* taking us to Hell," Atkins said.

Henry pushed himself to his feet, hugging the Book to his chest. "Whatever we're getting ourselves into down there, we need to be ready. No fucking around. No fighting each other. If we want to stay alive, and I suspect both of you do, we need to work together quickly and efficiently. Whatever these rituals are, it's clear this is well beyond anything any of us has experienced before. We *need* to survive."

As the others let his words sink in, the walls enclosing them disappeared, and the elevator descended into a cavernous chamber, lit sparsely by oil lanterns burning within walls of smooth, wet rock. Here and there the cavern was reinforced with stone masonry to prevent collapse.

"Don't look down," Henry said.

Atkins gripped the cage with both hands, nervously staring at the rock floor far below them. "*Jesus.*"

Henry spotted something stacked in the shape of a pyramid against the far wall. "What are those down there?"

"It looks like barrels," Joy said. She blinked rapidly. "I remember hearing stories about secret tunnels under L.A. when I was little. There's supposed to be miles and miles of them, pedestrian tunnels and subway tunnels and even old horse tunnels that are completely abandoned. I guess a lot of them were probably used during Prohibition, but I bet the majority of them were just forgotten. Also, there's this legend, you might've heard it, of a race of super-intelligent lizard people who supposedly lived under the city over five thousand years ago? An engineer—Shubert, I think his name was—dug these shafts into the ground and allegedly discovered a whole warren of tunnels and lost treasure down there... or here, I suppose."

"Shufelt," Henry said. "It's supposed to be under Fort Moore Hill. Or at least that's where I heard about it."

"Urban legend bullshit," Atkins said, looking queasy.

Joy rolled her eyes. "Bullshit or not, this looks a lot like an old cave, not something manmade. And if this was used during Prohibition as those barrels imply, that means the tunnels probably lead under the old doll factory across the street."

"*Dolls*," Atkins moaned. "I *hate* dolls."

Henry chuckled. "Yeah, I'm not a big fan either, I gotta say."

Joy shrugged. She seemed to be intrigued by what lay below them, and now that they were closer to the floor of the cavern Henry could see old wooden crates as well as the stacked barrels.

Eventually the elevator came to a jarring stop. Atkins jerked the door open and staggered out, panting heavily. Joy followed him, crossing the cavern floor. Henry stepped out last, tucking the Book back under an arm. The moment he did, the elevator car began to rise. He laid the Book down on the ground and grabbed at the floor of the elevator car. It kept rising, lifting him off his feet. He let go before the roof of the doorway could lop off his hands and fell to the ground, raising clouds of dirt.

"We lost the elevator," he called out, his voice echoing.

"Good riddance," Atkins grunted. "I wouldn't get back in that thing if you paid me."

Henry, on the other hand, worried it was their last mode of escape should they fail to solve whatever this next puzzle was in time. As it rose out of sight into the darkness above them, its rickety grumbling and groaning gave way to the sound of swiftly dripping water, echoing throughout the cavern.

The space they'd entered appeared to be a vaguely circular

chamber about twenty feet in diameter. The walls narrowed the higher up it went, creating the shape of a flattened teardrop.

"Looks like there was a cave-in here," Atkins said, still panting. He stood in front of what appeared to be a stone archway, completely covered with rocks. "Maybe we could dig our way out... if we had a hundred years."

"I found an old diagram," Joy said, standing near the triangular stack of barrels. "It looks like clothing sizes. *XL... L... XXL... C*? What's *C*? Children's? I think they correspond to the barrels, whatever it is." She shrugged. "Might just be a bunch of random letters, though."

Henry crossed to the nearest crates, more curious about those than the barrels, which he assumed from Joy's mention of Prohibition tunnels likely once contained whiskey and rum, possibly long since evaporated. If not, they'd be far more potent than they'd been a hundred years prior when they were casked.

The old crates were made of thin wooden slats, packing straw visible in the gaps between them. Each was stamped with the same words: PARTS CONFORM TO ORDERS OF THE WAR PRODUCTION BOARD.

"This doll factory," Henry said. "What happened to it, Joy? Do you know?"

She looked up from the diagram. "They converted it to make munitions during World War II, from what I read. The dollmaker got committed to Patton State Hospital around that time and the factory fell into ruin. The house stood in disrepair until the '70s or '80s when the city finally condemned it, but as far as I know the factory was never used again. I used to see rats skittering in and out of it all the time. Alexei jokingly called it the Kingdom of Rats, but I think he was secretly worried they'd end up infesting the house."

"Hmm," Henry said. Without a crowbar handy, he pried off slats with his bare hands. They snapped easily, brittle from age. He pulled away bunches of straw to reveal a nest of small metal canisters painted olive green.

SMOKELESS POWDER, they said.

Gunpowder.

"I think we might be able to clear that cave-in," he said.

THE FLOOD

T HAT SHIT IS seventy years old, Hall," Atkins scoffed. "Even if it is still good it won't explode. See there, it says 'smokeless powder;' i.e. it won't fucking blow up. They made it that way on purpose."

"I know that," Henry said, gently placing the cannister he'd taken out of the box back in its nest of straw. "It burns in open air. But if we can ignite it *inside* the cannister with the lid closed, it might build up enough pressure to explode. *Or…*"

Joy watched as he started pacing the cavern, reminding her of Ileana when she'd been plotting how to spin the death of Jessica Danvers to her advantage. She'd likely had to learn to spin horrible tragedies early, considering the alleged "hazing" incident she'd been involved in during college.

"Joy, lemme see that diagram," Henry said suddenly, turning and crossing to her. He put the Book down on the table where she'd found the diagram. She handed it to him.

Henry scanned the weathered document. "These are Roman numerals," he said finally. "They go up by tens. *X* to *C*. Ten to one hundred."

"Meaning what?"

Henry looked over the barrels, from one to the next. "They used to test the proof of alcohol by mixing it with gunpowder and seeing if it would burn. What if these numbers are proofs?"

"Why do you know so much about this shit, Hall?"

"I was a curious kid with an early affinity for alcohol."

Atkins chuckled. "Touché."

"But these symbols," Henry said, laying the diagram back down on the table and spreading it flat to point them out. "I have no idea what those are."

Joy looked over the images again. The same two were repeated, one in each of the numbered circles. Both of them looked like profile portraits of little bejeweled goblins, reminding Joy of drawings she'd seen a long time ago but couldn't place. One of them had a long nose and what looked like a horn or spigot in his headdress. The other seemed to be wearing a lot of bling and held a chalice. "These look familiar," she said, hoping to jog her memory. "Some kind of hieroglyph?"

Henry shook his head. "No clue."

"I guess we're fucked then," Atkins said with a sigh.

Joy wouldn't let the man bring her down. The only way to get out of this place was to stay positive, stay motivated. She crossed to the crate Henry had opened and regarded the old gunpowder cannisters. Something was tucked down between them, mostly hidden in the straw. "There's a sheet of paper in here." She reached between the cannisters, reminding herself of a scene from the first *Arrowheart* movie, where she'd had to reach into a crate filled with bombardier beetles to fish out an ancient emerald necklace. Thinking of this reminded her of Henry sticking his hand into the hole in the wall with the arrow pointing to it.

Now, you're getting out of here, he'd said. Not *we're* getting out of here. *You're*. He really had been prepared to sacrifice his own life to save the rest of them. He'd fully expected the lever that opened the door could have trapped him there, making him the next sacrifice.

Would I do the same for him? She wasn't sure. She'd only just met him, but she did feel as though they were connected in some way she couldn't understand. They were linked by Infiniti, but she felt it was more than that. She wondered if maybe they'd met before, or in some other life. It was silly but now that she'd thought it, the notion was unshakeable.

This could go far deeper than we know.

Pinching the fragile piece of paper between her middle and

forefinger, she managed to pull it out of its nest and looked it over.

It was an old typewritten instruction sheet, or at least made to *look* old. Across the top it said *INSTRUCTIONS FOR MIXING*. Below was a list of numbers from ten to one hundred, along with the same symbols as on the diagram. Underneath that, the symbols were explained with equal signs connected to vaguely familiar words. The little man with the cup equaled ITZAMNA. The guy with the spigot hat was CHAAHK. Whatever they meant it seemed less like instructions and more like another mystery.

Until the names and symbols clicked.

"Chaahk is the rain god," she said.

"How do you know that?" Atkins grunted.

"Helen Arrowheart."

Both men looked at her in confusion. She took a moment to marvel that she'd somehow managed to get stuck in what could possibly be her last moments alive with the only two people in the world who didn't know her most famous character.

"Oh, riiiight," Atkins said finally. "That *Tomb Raider* rip-off."

Joy scowled. "It's not a '*Tomb Raider* rip-off,'" she said with disdain. "They're an homage to Indiana Jones and the swashbuckling adventurers of the past."

"Whatever you say, sister."

Joy looked to Henry for support.

He shrugged. "I don't watch a lot of movies. I think I might have seen an ad for it, though. Online maybe."

"Anyway, it doesn't matter," she went on. "Chaahk is the Mayan god of rain and thunder. During pre-pro for *Arrowheart 2*, they sent us to Belize to do the Crystal Cave tour and Tikal in Guatemala, just to soak up as much about Mayan history as we could. I remember the tour guide told us Itzamna was the god of the sky or the heavens. A creator god. Maybe *the* creator god. She said archeologists used to call him 'god D' before they deciphered the names of the Mayan gods. She said his name probably came from the Yucatan word for 'sorcerer,' but earlier it was thought to be a combination of the words for 'lizard' and 'house.'"

"Lizard House," Atkins said. "Sounds like a National Lampoon movie."

Henry's eyebrows rose as he seemed to clue in to what Joy was suggesting. "Shufelt's Lizard People?"

"Maybe," she said, excited by the theory. "I don't think there's any record of the Mayans traveling this far north, but could it be possible? I know they experienced a prolonged drought, long enough that their priests went underground with giant clay pots, getting high on hallucinogens and praying to Chaahk to bring the rain. They even sacrificed a young boy they call the 'Crystal Maiden,' I guess because it was assumed that all human sacrifices were virginal girls, when we know now the Mayans mostly decapitated male prisoners of war. Even after doing all that, the drought collapsed their *entire civilization*. What if some of them lost their faith in the priests and Chaahk and migrated north to find a more temperate climate?"

"I don't know about all that," Henry said. "But I guess it's possible."

"So that's why the Mayans died off?" Atkins asked. "I thought it was the Spanish conquistadors bringing disease."

"They didn't *die off*. Lots of Mayan people still live in Mexico and all across Central America."

Henry pointed at the diagram, apparently having lost interest in the subject. "If these numbers are proofs," he said, "we might be able to mix the alcohol in those barrels with the gunpowder in these cannisters and make ourselves some homemade explosives. If we could get them placed strategically…"

"We could clear the rock jam!" Atkins came over and clapped Henry on the shoulder. "Hall, if you get us out of here,

I'll take back every single thing I ever said about you."

Henry regarded the shoulder Atkins touched as if it was crawling with bugs. "Let's not jerk each other off just yet."

"Okay, but the symbols have to mean *something*," Joy said. "This one says one hundred but it's got the symbol for Chaahk and this one has the symbol for Itzamna. And why is the X all by itself in the middle barrel? It's the only one without a symbol."

"X marks the spot?" Atkins suggested, shrugging.

Henry studied the barrels. "It could be... It might just be an empty barrel."

"Only one way to find out." Atkins stepped around the table to the stack of barrels. He reached up and turned the handle on the spigot. Nothing came out but a few grains of dirt. He knocked on the top of it, creating a hollow thump. "It's empty."

"What's in the other boxes?" Joy said. "How many cans of gunpowder would we need to clear that jam, you think?"

"I dunno, I didn't check. The six in the box would probably do, but we have to make sure it'll ignite with the alcohol. The higher the proof the better."

"So... C is one hundred, right? C should be the highest proof."

"Sure, theoretically. But you said yourself, the symbols have to be connected."

"Well, Chaahk is the rain god. Maybe it's liquid."

Henry considered it a moment, then nodded. "Yeah, maybe."

Atkins looked at the diagram, then returned to the barrels and twisted the corresponding handle. Clear liquid began pouring out, splashing on the rock floor between his boots. He stepped back and stuck a finger into the flow, then tasted it, smacking his lips. "It's water," he said.

"Water," Henry repeated.

The three of them looked at the running stream, clearly all thinking the same thing. It had been ages since they'd drank anything, but just like the water cooler back in the TV studio puzzle, it could easily be poison.

Joy almost considered drinking it anyway, her throat so dry

it felt raw.

When Atkins tried turning off the valve, the handle snapped off in his hand. He muttered, "Shit," as the water kept pouring out over the floor of the cavern. The puddle had already spread beyond the table legs. He stuck a thumb in the hole, holding the stream at bay. "Great, now I gotta stand here like the little boy and the dyke."

"Just let it pour itself out," Henry said.

Atkins shrugged and let it go. "It's your funeral."

"Try the one with Itz..." He turned to Joy, clearly having forgotten the name.

"Itzamna," she said.

"Right. Second row from the top on the right."

"Okay," Atkins said. He raised himself up on his tiptoes and the handle turned with a squeak. Liquid poured out, the color of gold. He did another finger test. This time his eyes widened as if he'd eaten a hot pepper. "Ooh, that's smooth!"

"'Smooth,'" Henry repeated with an amused grin. "All right, turn it off. We'll need to conserve it. Let's get the cannisters."

Joy delicately grabbed two of the cannisters, tucking one under an arm, then took a third. Henry came over, the Book left on the table, and did the same.

"They're not fragile," he said.

"I wasn't sure if it was like old dynamite."

"Nah. Good catch, by the way. The Mayan god stuff. I never would've thought of that. We'd still be turning those faucets on and off trying to find the right one if you hadn't figured that out."

She grinned. "Let's not jerk each other off just yet."

Henry laughed. Giving her a serious look, he spoiled their moment of levity. "We're gonna make it out of here."

"I know," she said, though the only thing she knew for sure was that this house had been a death trap long before her estranged husband gutted it, remodeling the remains to suit his eclectic taste. If these caves really were the lost city of Shufelt's so-called Lizard People, whether they'd been nomadic Mayans, strayed members of a local tribe, or some alien race from the far reaches of the galaxy, it was likely they'd never made it out of this place alive.

It was just as likely she and the others wouldn't, either.

"I wish I could've seen him one last time," she said as they carried the cannisters to the table.

"Who? Oh, your ex. Yeah."

"I'd just would've liked to tell him to his face how much he disappointed me. How awful he made me feel in those last few years we spent together." She chuckled ruefully, reminded of something from a long time ago. "You know he made me sign an NDA before we got married?"

"You mean a prenup?"

"No, a literal NDA, stating I wouldn't reveal anything that might occur during our marriage."

"That's... is that even legal?" Henry placed his cannisters on the table and began unscrewing the lids. Joy did the same. Atkins watched them. She knew he was likely listening to every word of their conversation, but she didn't care. Alexei was dead. She figured that voided any NDA she could've ever been asked to sign.

"I don't know. He had his little weasel of a lawyer come to my condo in a white linen suit the night before our wedding."

"A lawyer. Was his name... Brent Foxworth?"

"Trent." She looked up, midway through unscrewing the last cap which appeared to be mostly rusted shut. "How did you know that?"

"Lucky guess," he said with a shrug. "I wonder..."

"What?"

"If any of the others signed NDAs with that guy."

"I dunno. But I *do* know Jessica Danvers signed his college acceptance form."

"That's three out of six. I'm willing to bet that lawyer of his is deeply connected to Infiniti Enterprises."

"Wouldn't surprise me in the least." She held up the cannister she'd been working on. "I can't get this one open."

"Rap it on the table," Henry suggested.

She did. When she tried again it opened easily.

"Just like magic," Henry said with a smile. "I used to tell Clara, my daughter, that it really was magic. Had her believing it until she was… twelve, maybe?"

Joy smiled. "I'm sorry," she said.

"It's okay. If anything, today's made me realize I've been putting too much energy into grieving for her. Hell, I'll be in prison for thirteen more years even if I do happen to get out of this place, which at this point is highly unlikely."

She nodded somberly. Atkins uttered a bitter laugh.

"Clara's murder tore my entire life apart. It destroyed our marriage. Instead of being there for Mercy, my wife, I've been locked away for the past two years while she's had to work through all of this on her own." He shook his head, biting his lower lip. "But I was locked up in my own head well before they threw me in jail. You're lucky you hated him, Joy. *Grief is a prison*," he said, offering her a sad smile. "The key is in your mind."

Joy considered his words. If anyone understood the stranglehold grief could have over a person's life, it was a man facing another decade in solitary confinement. No wonder he'd been willing to give up his life for them. How much hope did he have even if they did manage to survive these final puzzles?

"Better test this first," he said. He turned to Atkins. "You still have my lighter?"

"Yeah," Atkins said, seemingly lost in thought. He fished into the right pocket of his slacks and brought out a shiny silver Zippo. "Don't blow up the place."

Henry took the lighter. "Not yet," he said. Crouching before the barrels, he lit the Zippo and held the flame to the small puddle of liquor on the ground. It burned with a blue flame. "It's good. Let's give it a try."

Joy handed him a cannister. He held it under the correct barrel and twisted the handle. "Here goes nothing…"

Amber liquid poured into the cannister, glugging at a higher pitch until it reached the mouth, where Henry turned off the spigot. "We need some of that straw."

"I'll grab some," Joy said. She hurried to the crates, but some instinct drew her to the unopened ones beside it. She peered through the slats, seeing small dark shadows within. Pulling on the thin boards, snapping them, she revealed its contents.

Heads.

She gasped, then realized what she was looking at: six pale mannequin heads lay within the bed of straw, a dozen painted blue eyes staring up at her. Joy shuddered, recalling these same faces following her progress as she'd skirted down the aisle in the studio audience to fetch the gas mask. Looking over the other boxes, she pictured torsos and limbs all separated from one another, ready to be shipped to department stores that likely no longer existed.

Not wanting to disturb them—wondering if the ones in the studio had been animated with robotics or by some kind of dark magic—she returned to the crate Henry had opened and grabbed a handful of straw. When she got back to the table, Henry was popping holes in the lids with one of the lockpicking tools.

"You're a regular MacGyver," Atkins said.

Henry held out a hand. "Give me some straw. Three or four pieces."

Joy picked out four long pieces and handed them to Henry. "I guess I did most of my grieving for Alexei once we separated," she said as Henry twisted the straw through the small puncture, like threading a needle. "But a part of me still loved him, still wished he could've been turned around, that if I could've kept him safe from his ambition, he would've been the same man I married. I realized that today. While we were dating he told me, 'I will give you the world.' He *promised* me that, so many times. I just thought it was something romantic to say. But you know, a few weeks after we returned from our honeymoon, I got offered a part in the first *Arrowheart* movie. And it only got better and bigger from there. The same happened for him. We joked that we made each other whole. Now I have to wonder if I really did get where I am because of hard work and dedication to my craft, or if Infiniti wasn't pulling the strings behind the scenes the whole time."

"You put in the work, either way," Henry said. He held up the first bomb, with its cap in place and its wick of straw. "You ready to try this?"

She nodded eagerly. "Let's do it."

The three of them crossed the cavern to the cave-in. It looked impenetrable, almost as though each massive boulder and rock and stone had been mortared into place. Fortunately, there were small crevasses here and there, some large enough to fit one or even two of the cannisters. Henry found one close to the middle and slipped the bomb into it, the wick sticking out.

"You're gonna want to stand back," he said over his shoulder. Then he shrugged. "If we're lucky."

Atkins crossed his fingers and stepped back alongside her. Henry, meanwhile, flicked the wheel on his lighter. The straw caught fire, small and yellow. The flame threatened to die out and Henry blew on it, causing it to smolder before catching again and burning its way up the straw.

Henry ran back to where they stood and covered his ears. Joy and Atkins did the same.

The flame licked its way up to the lid with a sweet smoky smell but fizzled out again rather than continue through the hole he'd poked into it. Henry took his hands off his ears. Joy could barely hear him curse.

With a surprisingly loud bang the cannister exploded in a ball of flame, and Henry clapped his hands to his ears a moment too late. The explosion echoed throughout the chamber as bits of rock and shredded tin rained down between them and the cave-in.

Atkins grinned, lowering his hands. "Not bad, Hall."

A deep rumble from somewhere beyond the cave-in shook the ground beneath their feet. Joy peered around anxiously as the barrels rocked in their frame and two of the five remaining cannisters toppled over on the table.

"What was that?" she gasped.

"Earthquake?" Atkins suggested.

They'd all spent enough time in Southern California to be very familiar with tremors. Joy had heard there were something like thirty a day throughout the area, though most of them were so minor they couldn't be felt. She wondered if Henry or Atkins had been this far underground during one before, and didn't imagine it was likely.

"I don't think—" was all Henry managed, before a jet of water spewed forth from the hole he'd created.

"Oh, you gotta be fucking kidding me!" Atkins shouted over the gush of water. "There's your fuckin rain god!"

A second resounding boom caused several of the larger rocks and boulders to tumble into the cavern, and the narrow spray of water became a literal geyser, pouring over their feet.

"We need to find higher ground," Henry said over the din that had risen in volume to a small waterfall.

Joy looked up to where the elevator cage disappeared into the darkness. If they managed to open the cage, they could ride the rising water up the shaft. But that would put them right back where they'd started, in the corridor with those mindless zombie cultists.

The pressure of the water pouring from the opening would make it impossible to squeeze through. If they couldn't find an exit they were dead, all three of them.

Joy glanced over at the table.

"We need to save the papers!" she shouted, making a run for it. She scooped up the diagram and "Instructions for Mixing," then wondered if they hadn't been tricks all along. *Was blowing up the cave-in a... a whatchacallit? A red herring?*

"*X* marks the spot!" she called out over the noise.

Looking excited, Henry splashed through ankle-deep water to reach her. "Which barrel was that?"

She looked over the diagram. "Third row from the top in the middle."

"The eight ball," he said. He trudged over to the barrels and reached up to turn the handle Atkins had turned earlier.

Rather than add yet another stream of liquid to their growing misery, the lid fell open on a hidden hinge.

Henry peered into the barrel. "There's light coming from here!"

"It's an opening?" Atkins waded over, the water up to his knees and rising fast, with more large rocks tumbling out of the cave-in.

Joy climbed up on the table and stood shakily to get a look inside the opened barrel. Henry was right. An orange glow flickered off the wall of what looked like a ten to fifteen-foot tunnel through the back of the barrel. *Candles? Torchlight?*

"There's another room back there!"

"Wait," Atkins said, looking anxious. "We all know it's just gonna be another trap. If the water keeps rising, it's like a bathtub overflow. We could just wait it out on top of the barrels. Sooner or later, someone is gonna have to come down here to clean up the mess."

"Depends on the pressure differential," Henry said.

"The what?"

"The Bernoulli effect. With the speed the water is rising out here they could've made this exit in a way that the water will keep rising regardless of any outflow. Meaning, by the time we know anything for sure we'll have to dive to reach this opening."

Atkins looked to Joy for confirmation, but all she could offer was a confused shrug. She knew very little about science beyond high school, and figured Henry had needed to know a little bit about everything to be any good at his job, unless he'd relied solely on gut instinct.

Atkins gritted his teeth and punched the surface of the water at his hips. "Fuck this house! And fuck Alexei fucking Vaseline!"

"Vasiliev," Joy said as the table started to wobble under her feet with the water beginning to lift it. "If we're planning on getting out of here, we should get moving. This table's about to float away."

"Okay," Henry said. "I'll go first. I'll make sure the way is clear. All right?"

"Joy should go first," Atkins grunted.

Joy shook her head. As badly as she wanted to get out of here, it was clear Henry was their leader.

"Well, I'm sure as fuck not going first," Atkins grunted.

Joy nodded. "Just go, Henry," she said. "We'll be right behind you."

Henry gave her a nod and grabbed the bottom of the barrel.

He got a foothold on the rack's frame below and to the right of it, then pulled himself up, slipping headfirst into the opening.

"It's a tight squeeze," he said from within, his voice echoing hollowly.

"I'm next," Atkins said, shooting her a glare.

Joy nodded for him to go on, rocking on the tabletop, riding it like a surfboard. If they waited much longer the water would rise above the opening and they'd have to dive, like Henry had said. She'd done plenty of diving in her career, especially as Helen Arrowheart. But she would've preferred to avoid it if possible. Who knew what kinds of things were floating in this water? It didn't *smell* like sewage, but she'd rather not take her chances.

Imagine surviving all of this just to come out with a staph infection or ringworm.

The thought made her cringe.

Atkins climbed clumsily into the barrel and started crawling on his knees and elbows, his silhouette outlined by the orange flicker of distant flames.

"Now or never," Joy said, psyching herself up. Without waiting a beat she leaped off the table, grabbing hold of the top barrel. With her parkour training she managed to swing her legs through the opening in a single, almost graceful move. She rolled onto her stomach, just as the cool water rose over the lip of the barrel, realizing all too late that her entrance, graceful or not, meant she would have to crawl backwards through the tunnel.

"Everyone okay in here?" she called, beginning to scurry backwards as her voice echoed behind her.

"All good," Henry shouted from a distance. "There's a ladder here."

"Speak for yourself," Atkins said, closer to her.

As she entered the smooth rock tunnel behind the barrel, she heard Henry's footfalls on the ladder. The water was already covering her lower legs as she sloshed through it. In another minute the entire tunnel would be filled to the top and she'd have to hold her breath.

"Oh, thank Christ," Atkins said behind her. A moment later

she heard him begin climbing the ladder. "Move your ass, Hall."

"Is Joy coming?" Henry asked, his voice not much further away.

"I'm here," she shouted.

Finally, the tunnel opened up behind her. She climbed out and stood in water up to her shins, relieved to be able to turn her head and see where she was going. Firelight flickered off the walls from above. Atkins stood about ten feet up the rusty, rickety-looking ladder. Henry was near the opening, maybe another ten feet higher. The flames were much brighter, burning like the corona of an eclipse around Henry's silhouette, reminding her of the sun-eating god in his Book.

She grabbed the rung just above her head and started climbing. The sound of rushing water trailed off as she ascended and for several moments the only sound was the clunk of their shoes and boots on the rusted metal, followed by the scuffle of Henry's shoes on sandy rock.

"Holy shit," Henry said. "Holy fucking shit."

"What? What is it, Hall?"

"You gotta see this."

Joy looked up as Atkins climbed through the opening and disappeared. "Jeeee-*zus*," he said. "Is that *real gold*?"

"I think so."

Atkins's whistle echoed down the tunnel.

No wonder it's so bright, she thought. *It's not just the flames, it's firelight reflecting off of gold.*

Joy climbed faster, eager to witness the treasure they'd discovered. It was just like something out of an *Arrowheart* film. They'd solved all of the puzzles and survived every fiendish booby trap, and now they'd receive the spoils of their efforts.

I will give you the world.

Could this be what Alexei had meant? Had he really been good to his word, for once in his miserable life?

Joy was so close she could smell the fire from the treasure chamber, along with a whiff of accelerant. She climbed up and into a short horizontal tunnel. Henry watched her with a relieved smile. She returned it, crawling toward him. It was just as he said: torches flickered in a chamber shimmering with gold. It was *everywhere*, from the arches of the vaulted ceiling to the altar directly behind him, with ornate sculptural reliefs and cuneiform covering every square inch of its magnificent surface and three golden bowls resting upon it, the center bowl holding a guttering flame.

She poked her head into the chamber with a victorious laugh, half expecting a camera crew to be awaiting her arrival, the triumphant return of Helen Arrowheart, last of the old school treasure hunters. As she began crawling out, Atkins stepped between her and Henry, wearing a vicious sneer. He reached out to the left of the exit as if to switch on a light.

Joy reacted a moment too late. She heard a metallic *snick!* which could have been a paparazzi's camera or the sound of a blade scraped against whetstone. With an intense burst of pain at the back of her neck, darkness descended over her.

The spotlight never returned.

THE ALTAR

HENRY DIDN'T EVEN have a moment to call out to Joy before the heavy blade descended on her like a clapboard's clapper, severing her head cleanly at the nape of the neck. Her head ejected out of the hole like a ball fired from a cannon and he caught it, pulling it in to his chest. Her wide eyes, brimming with excitement and relief just moments ago, stared up at him in eternal horror, her teeth clenched in a pained rictus.

"And… *scene*," Atkins said, chuckling to himself.

"What the fuck!" Henry cried, tossing Joy's head away in revulsion. It landed with a wet thud and rolled until it lay face down in a halo of her wavy hair. Twin jets of blood squirted weakly from the severed arteries, then ceased. "*Jesus fucking Christ, Atkins, what the fuck?*"

Atkins didn't reply, merely bent nonchalantly as if to tie his boots. Eight severed fingers lay scattered at his feet in their own spatters of blood. Henry nearly rushed him in his rage—it was obvious he'd deliberately triggered some kind of mechanism to drop the blade on her—but reconsidered when Atkins stood and turned, grinning wide, a small pistol gripped in his right hand. He must have kept the second gun, likely a .22-caliber, in an ankle holster.

Henry felt like a fool for not assuming the man might be keeping a backup gun. Many of his fellow detectives did the same, though most considered holding them in an ankle holster insecure. Apparently Atkins had no issue with them. He had to give the man props for acting his ass off when he'd thrown his sidearm down the hole.

"Of all fucking people it could've been, it had to be you, didn't it?" the prick grunted.

"Why the fuck did you do that?"

"You said it yourself, Hall. These are rituals. Rituals require sacrifices." He stooped again, still holding the gun on Henry, and picked up Joy's head by the hair.

"You sick fuck."

"Yeah, that's right, Hall. I *am* a sick fuck." He crossed toward the altar of gold, keeping an eye on Henry and the weapon trained on him. "A sick fuck who's about to join his friends to rule a whole new world. See, I figured it would either be you or her come the end of this thing. Those others didn't have the sack for it." He shrugged. "Eh, maybe Ileana did, if she wasn't still so concerned with that silly little thing in her past. But *you two...*"

Atkins deposited Joy's head in one of two golden bowls on either side of the fire bowl. Her wide, lifeless eyes stared in the vague direction of the blade that had ended her life. Henry had a feeling he knew what the other empty bowl was meant for, and he didn't plan to let that happen if he could prevent it.

"*...you two* have survivor's instincts. When you took the Grimoire, when you recognized its *significance*, and when Joy held Oscar's bladder in her hands... I knew I'd end up right here with one of you." He regarded Joy's head and shrugged with one shoulder. "One and a half," he corrected himself.

"You're gonna pay for this," Henry said through gritted teeth, clenching his jaw in impotent fury.

"No, Hall. I won't. Don't you get it? The old rules don't apply anymore. Murder is back in fashion. Hell, you could walk outta here a free man if it were up to me. Sadly, for you, we've got one last ritual to perform." He gestured with his free hand. "Gimme the book."

"Why would I do that?"

"Because if you don't, I'll shoot you in the gut. Let you bleed out instead of a quick, relatively painless bullet to the head." He gestured toward Joy. "You think she *suffered*, Hall? She was *smiling* when it happened. Just a flash of pain and lights out. Isn't that how we'd all prefer to shuffle off this mortal fucking coil? Of course, I'll be immortal soon. So will all my friends, Servants of the Great Watcher in the Sky, hallowed be thy fucking name. So hand over the Book, Hall. Make it easy on yourself."

"Fuck you," Henry said.

Atkins called his bluff with a twitch of his finger.

The *pop* was deafening in the small space. The slug struck Henry on his right side, burning a searing hole in his abdomen just below the ribs. He regarded the wound, a gout of dark blood pouring from it, and laughed in awe. It hurt like hell, but he doubted it had hit any vital organs.

Then he tossed the Book.

It sailed past Atkins's dismayed face. The man swiped at it with his free hand, then chased after it like an outfielder believing he could catch it in the stands. He missed, sprawling over the altar. The Book landed in the fire bowl and instantly ignited. Atkins shrieked and pulled it out of the flames. With his back turned to him, Henry kicked him in the ass, sending him sprawling over the altar once more. Atkins managed to hold on to the Book, but he lost the gun. It clattered on the floor somewhere behind the altar. The smell of burning flesh prickled his nostrils, reminding him of the apartment fire in Long Beach all those years ago.

"You fuck!" Atkins cried. Desperate to put out the flames, he battered the Book against the altar, knocking over the leftmost bowl. Joy's head tumbled out with a dull thud.

With this final disrespect, Henry lost it. He grabbed Atkins by the hair and shoved his face toward the fire bowl. Atkins fought back, dropping the Book and elbowing him, the blow hitting Henry right in the bullet wound.

Henry staggered back, the wind knocked out of him.

Atkins threw up his fists, the left blackened with soot, and advanced on him. "I'm gonna enjoy this, Hall."

He threw a hook. Henry ducked it and returned it with a jab, catching Atkins in the chin. The man shook his head and kept coming, swinging again, catching Henry in the injured side, his fist coming back bloody. Henry stumbled back another two steps. The wall was three, maybe four feet behind him, the hole level with his hips.

He couldn't let Atkins back him into it.

He took two belabored steps to the side. "Only one of us is getting out of here, Atkins. It's not gonna be you."

Atkins grinned, his teeth stained with blood. "What makes you think that?"

Henry tapped his temple. "Because I have the key," he said, covertly reaching into his back pocket with the hand he'd been holding against his wound.

"You *are* the key, Hall," Atkins said. "The second your scumbag fucking head goes in that bowl, I'm free."

Henry uttered a single laugh. "Then come get it."

Atkins roared and threw himself at Henry. As they collided, Henry grabbed the walk-in fridge key from his pocket and shoved it forward with all of his strength. The pointed end struck Atkins in just about the same place the bullet had hit Henry. Atkins cried out and pushed Henry back until his head struck the wall. Stars momentarily shot across his vision, but he held firm to the back of the man's neck, pulling Atkins toward him while dragging the tool upwards. Atkins bellowed as flesh and fabric tore with a wet ripping sound, and when the tool struck his bottom rib Henry finally let the man free. Atkins careened backwards, falling on his ass against the altar. Peering down at the bleeding gash in his side, a bastardized version of the holy wound Pontius Pilate had inflicted upon Jesus, he laughed.

"We're twins," he grunted. Then he pushed himself up and lurched across the chamber, raising his fists again: the right smeared with blood, the left still black from soot.

Lacking brute force, the lockpick wasn't a good enough weapon, not to kill a man. They were likely about even weight-wise, but Atkins had a few inches on him and a longer reach. Prison had weakened Henry. He'd never spent a moment in the gym, had used up all his time grieving, painting and reading. It was unlikely he could kill the man with his bare hands. Atkins wouldn't stop until he was dead. He'd suffered through each of the puzzle rooms like the rest of them, at times working at odds with them. It was clear he had the motivation and the wherewithal to fight until one or the other of them was dead. And the gun was hidden somewhere on the floor behind the altar.

As his nemesis staggered forward Henry heard a steady drip behind him. He looked down to see Joy's fingers floating past his wet shoes in a growing pool of water.

The tunnel's still filling up!

With Atkins almost upon him, Henry scoured the wall for the lever or button to control the blade. He found what he thought might be it—a small divot a few inches to the left of the hole—and rushed for it.

Atkins clocked what he was attempting and launched himself at him, slamming him into the wall. Henry's hip and the bullet wound bashed into the protruding stone lip of the tunnel. In his agony he dropped the lockpick—it skittered out of sight across the floor—but he managed to reach up and grab Atkins by the throat with his right hand. Atkins reared back and headbutted him, causing another spray of fireworks to dance in front of Henry's eyes. His momentary distraction allowed Atkins to grab him around the throat and drag him down to the floor, where the two of them knelt beside the opening, throttling each other to death with their bare hands.

"*Face the inevitable, Hall,*" Atkins choked. "*It'll be so much easier if you just die now! This world has no place for men like you!*"

"Fuck... *you,*" Henry groaned. He thrust a knee into Atkins's wound. Atkins cried out but didn't release his grip. Henry felt himself getting weaker by the second. After all they'd been through today, he was already on his last legs.

He glanced to his right. The divot was within reach. He just had to hope that he hadn't misjudged. The blade trembled against the pressure building up behind it.

He struck Atkins with another knee to the wound. The man's grip slackened but not enough for Henry to break free. He let go of Atkins's throat with his right hand and reached blindly for the divot. Atkins saw what he was doing and let go with his right, reaching over his left, still gripped around

166

Henry's larynx, to stop him from pressing the button.

Atkins grabbed his wrist. They struggled at neck and wrists, a dance of death. "You open that door, we'll both die," Atkins warned him.

"I *told* you," Henry spat, "I don't give a *shit* if I live or die. All I care is that *you don't fucking win.*"

Henry pulled against Atkins's grip with all his remaining might and determination. His palm slapped against the wall and he roamed its grainy surface until his fingertips reached the divot. Then he pushed.

Behind him, the blade rose with a razor sharp *shick!*

He didn't expect the deluge it released. Neither did Atkins. The man's eyes and mouth went wide as the blast of water struck them like a giant firehose, sending them both careening against the altar. Immediately the chamber began filling with water.

Soaked to the bone, battered, tired, Henry pushed himself up from the floor. Atkins had struck the altar headfirst, apparently. Diluted blood dripped down his forehead and the cut above his eye had opened afresh, adding to the gore. His life was ebbing away with each movement, pouring from the wounds in his scalp and abdomen. He blinked away the blood with a dazed look and staggered to his feet.

Henry lurched punch-drunk toward Chaahk's angry god-mouth, spewing cool water into the chamber. Already it was ankle-deep, slowing his progress. Soon this room and everything in it would be fully submerged. Henry doubted he could swim against the tide. His only option was to drop the blade again and hope he'd softened Atkins enough to get the upper hand.

As he thought this, Atkins struck him from behind, pushing him face-first into the water blast. He choked and gasped, the force of it making it impossible to close his mouth, impossible to breathe, his nostrils, eyes and ears filled with liquid, both blinding and deafening him. He reached back, hands scrabbling feebly at his attacker. Atkins held him under, shoving him forward against the flood until his chin pressed against wet stone.

In one movement Atkins could reach out and drop the blade, beheading him in an instant. The only thing that stopped him was Henry continuing to struggle. He was drowning. With every moment engulfed, with his lungs burning from disuse, his body continued to weaken. His pulse throbbed in his temples, slower by the second. He knew he couldn't keep it up for much longer.

He thought about his painting of Clara, covering the message scratched into the wall, the prayer to Nungal or whatever it was meant to be. Other than his desire not to let Atkins win, what was he fighting for? To spend the next thirteen years of his life in prison? To live a life where he could no longer see his daughter again?

I'll be with you soon, pumpkin, he thought.

Then he stopped fighting.

As Henry's body slackened, Atkins stopped shoving for barely an instant, either in triumph or merely relieved to no longer have to struggle. Whatever the reason, it gave Henry a brief window to twist slightly and throw a Hail Mary punch at Atkins's midsection.

The man stumbled back a step, giving Henry just enough slack to wrench out from under him and turn his face away from the surge. Sucking in a great gasp of air, he lunged up and grabbed Atkins by the shoulders, throwing him against the side of the tunnel. Atkins's head struck the stone and his eyelids fluttered as if he was about to lose consciousness.

Henry didn't give him any time to recover. He pushed him into the overflow, leveling his neck with the blade.

"Nungal sends her regards," he said, and pressed the button.

Atkins regained consciousness just long enough for shock to register on his face, distorted under the rush of rippling water. Then his head and the top inch or two of his neck vanished behind the plunging blade. His now headless body slid out of the opening, gouts of his blood mingling with the hip-deep water. Henry let go of the dead man's polo and the corpse sank languidly below the surface.

Henry dropped to his knees, panting, in agony, the water up to his shoulders. He sat there for several moments, wondering what to do next, whether he should even bother attempting to escape or just raise the blade and let the water take him, bleed out from the bullet wound, or both. He had to admit, the latter options sounded tempting. He'd been ready to give up his life for the others in the office puzzle, sticking his hand into that hole in the wall with little regard for his own wellbeing, half expecting something inside it to clamp down and lock him in place. What prevented him from just letting go now? What did he have to live for?

I still have Mercy. At least I think I do. I need to call her, if I ever get out of this fucking place.

It was this that got him up and moving, the thought of potentially seeing his wife one last time. Their marriage had strained after Clara's death and the trial and prison sentence had stretched them to the limit. She still took his collect calls, and listened patiently as he told her about life behind bars, but stories of her own life in the outside world had to be pulled out of her, and her visits had become less frequent, every couple of months instead of every few weeks. He'd started to wonder if he'd already lost her.

I could fight to get her back.

The first step was getting out of this chamber. What was it Atkins had said? *The second your scumbag fucking head goes in that bowl, I'm free.*

Standing to the side of the opening, he pressed the button once more. The blade shot up on a torrent of water, and Atkins's head hurtled out with it. Henry dropped the blade again, stemming the flow, and fumbled in his first attempt to grab the head. It floated away like a bobbing apple. He waded for it and managed to grab it by the hair, lifting it out of the water, relishing the look of horror etched forever onto his former rival's face.

"You know you're almost tolerable this way," he told the head, carrying it to the altar. Somehow the flames still guttered in the center bowl, unaffected by the water rising around it. He deposited the head into the bowl to its right, then picked up Joy delicately by the cheeks, feeling a pang of guilt at having to desecrate her body in order to perform the final ritual, whatever it might be. He set her down gently, closed her eyes, and reached for the Book. It was partly burned but not terribly damaged. It smelled like charred flesh, making him wonder if it hadn't been bound centuries ago in human skin.

"Now what?" he asked Atkins's head.

The man didn't reply. Henry would've been concerned if he had.

With no other ideas, he opened the Book and flipped through it to the final pages. The second and third to last pages were taken up with what he imagined were Mayan hieroglyphs and the two gods on either side, water pouring from the spigot of Chaahk and fiery rays of sunshine blasting from the sky around Itzamna. The creator god sat cross-legged on a platform surrounded by drowning men, with a bowl of human heads resting before him.

A flash of color drew Henry's attention from the Book. The flames in the bowl had begun to bloom, turning blue. He realized the blood from both heads was dripping down channels and mingling in the fire bowl. As the fire rose, the walls of the chamber began to rumble. Dust rained from the ceiling. Henry ducked, peering around anxiously, covering his head with the Book. After everything he'd been through today it would have been just his luck to die in another cave-in.

But the walls weren't crumbling. A portion of the wall behind the altar was actually *ascending*, revealing a bright, unnatural light beyond. The water level fell immediately, pouring through the opening. As the stone door rose above the height of the altar, he saw it had opened a passage into another elevator, this one far more modern, sleek with chrome and mirrors. His own reflection stared back at him, haggard, beaten, tired. His clothes were drenched with water and blood, his hair a tangled wet mop.

Henry stepped around the altar.

He saw the water was pouring into the space between the elevator and the stone chamber, into what was likely a long, dark shaft. The floor of the elevator itself was damp but not flooded. Atkins's pistol lay in a puddle inside.

Henry entered the elevator. He grabbed the handrail and

bent with a groan to pick up the gun, reminded of Oscar bending to tie his shoe in the morgue. He lifted his shirt and tucked the weapon swiftly into the blood-stained waistband of his pants.

"Congratulations, Henry," came a voice he'd never expected to hear again, startling him into rising too quickly, causing a spurt of blood to spill down his belly. He looked up to see a curved screen above the doors just as they began to slide shut. Two men he recognized stood against a backdrop of pure darkness.

One of them was Alexei Vasiliev, alive and well and smiling alongside his companion.

The man who'd spoken was Trent Foxworth.

THE END

HENRY STARED IN disbelief at the men on the
screen as the elevator swiftly ascended, giving
him a moment of vertigo and queasiness.

"I'm sure you are quite disoriented at the
moment," Alexei Vasiliev said, "your mind filled with so many
conflicting emotions. Perhaps you suffer from a touch of
survivor's guilt, as well? Understandable. I must admit, I had
hoped it would be Joy. I would have liked to ask her about the
man she'd paid to follow me. What did he intend to do, I
wonder? Alas, someone was very clearly in your corner.
Someone very powerful. Someone, perhaps, *not human.*"

Nungal, Henry thought. *Ruler of the underworld. Protector
of prisoners.*

Another thought followed this, his rational mind cutting in:
*These men have lost their minds. Playing games with people's
lives in the service of gods that don't even exist. This right here
is what happens when you have more money than sense.*

"Irregardless," Foxworth cut in, "a deal is a deal. You won
the game fair and square, and far be it from Infiniti Enterprises
to back out on a deal."

"Fuck you," Henry said, doubtful they could hear him. But
Foxworth surprised him by grinning.

"You see?" he asked his partner. "This is why I put my
money on Henry. You owe me half a million dollars."

Alexei chuckled. "Come find us if you're able, Henry." He
smiled his businessman's smile. "I believe you know where
we'll be."

Juno Tower, Henry thought but didn't say. *A half hour drive from here to Long Beach with late afternoon traffic. Seven- or eight-hours' walk. Not that Moore will let me get further than the sidewalk before she gets the wrist shackles back on me.*

"We have much to celebrate," the puzzle master went on, while his companion poured from a bottle of Dom Perignon into two long-stemmed glasses. "A new world, for instance. You'll discover the one you left behind has changed somewhat during your trials. It won't be easy to navigate. And of course, we must ring in the new year."

New year? Henry thought. *It's the middle of spring....*

Alexei took the champagne glass Foxworth offered and clinked it against his companion's. The men drank their contents in two gulps. While Foxworth refilled the glasses, Alexei said, "We welcome you to Year Zero, Henry. *The Watcher* welcomes you." Again, he offered that phony smile as he accepted his refilled glass. Raising it, as if to toast Henry, he said, "We'll see you tonight. Whether you come to accept your winnings or take revenge... we'll be waiting for you just the same."

As the men clinked glasses once more, the image cut to black.

In the next moment the elevator dinged. The doors slid open on the darkened interior of an abandoned building, the air redolent with the scent of dust, mold, machine oil and stale rat turds. Henry's mind filled in the details. They had traveled deep underground, entered the tunnels below Puzzle House and crossed under the old doll factory. Had the tunnels and altar chamber existed before the Infiniti cult appropriated it for their rituals, as Joy's story of the Lizard People suggested? Had the dollmakers themselves built this place *knowing* what lay below them?

A resounding *BOOM* rattled the building's foundation, loosing dust and small chunks of cement from above. The elevator squeaked and rocked, and Henry stepped out quickly, despite the sudden feeling he'd be safer inside.

"That sounded like an explosion," he said aloud. His own voice creeped him out in the vast open darkness of the factory.

173

Old machinery and scavenged wires littered the space between crumbling columns struggling to hold up the floor above. He could see right through a ragged hole in the second floor and the ceiling above it to the sky and what he saw troubled him.

It was full dark.

He glanced at his watch. The second hand still ticked away but the time showed just past two-thirty, much too early for night to have fallen. Worse, large birds circled the black sky like buzzards awaiting his demise.

You'll discover the one you left behind has changed somewhat during your trials, Alexei had said. What did he mean by that? And what was that explosion? Riots? Home-grown terrorists?

Henry limped across the concrete floor, navigating the detritus left behind by decades of squatters and junkies and drunks. When he got to the front doors he remembered seeing they were chained shut from the outside when he'd arrived at the house. He wouldn't make it out this way.

He took off his shirt and cinched it around his abdomen, hoping to stem the flow of blood from his wound until Moore could get him fixed up with the med kit in the van. Leaning against the doors a moment, he breathed through a wave of pain. Then he crossed to the broken cinderblock he'd spotted on his way across the factory floor, stooped with a wince to pick it up, and brought it to the closest paned window. He hurled it through unceremoniously. The glass shattered, much of the rotted frame falling with the shards. The rest he cleared away with a rusty piece of rebar and tossed it behind him. It landed with an echoing clang.

Carefully, he pulled himself over the ledge and without causing himself too much agony managed to land in the tall grass outside. Crickets chirped. The city around him was unnaturally dark. The house across the street stood like a black obelisk against the darksome sky, its rooms without light.

Must be a blackout, he thought. *Citywide or just this neighborhood?*

Despite the early nightfall Henry still found it quite hot, almost like standing next to a furnace. He craned his neck to look up at the sky above him. The large birds still circled menacingly. And though it was seemingly cloudless, the sky itself was darker than he'd ever seen it. Having grown up in L.A. he was used to not seeing stars at night outside of a few key spots. Still, with the loss of electricity he would have expected to see a satellite zipping by, at least.

But there was nothing, almost as if the stars themselves no longer burned in the unforgiving cold of space.

That's weird, he thought, and got moving.

He had to break the chains on the fence with another piece of rebar, jamming it through and rotating it until the rusty links snapped. He shouldered open the gate and staggered out over the broken asphalt to the road.

The van looked strange, almost as though the back of it had been crushed by a giant hand.

"Moore?" he called out.

He looked both ways down the street. To the left of the factory was an overgrown field and the silhouette of the city. A car burned about half a block down the street to the right. He'd seen it when they arrived, figured it must have belonged to either Joy or Oscar. It belonged to no one anymore. He wondered if that had been the source of the explosion he'd heard as the elevator doors opened. It had sounded much louder though, like a refinery blowing up.

A dark shape shrieked behind him as it swooped down from overhead. Henry ducked as the shadow, caught in the firelight, swam across the road to his left. He watched the creature—it was clear it wasn't a bird from the size and shape of it—as it landed awkwardly on the top of the house, perching like a stone gargoyle. The shape was hulking and humanoid, aside from its wings, the massive paws and elongated head. Its eyes burned blood red, the same as the insane cultists' who'd killed Ileana inside the house.

Gallu, Henry thought with a shudder. *Prison guards of the Mesopotamian underworld. Fuck me, they were right. The world has changed.*

Periodically glancing up at the other gallu circling the sky, he staggered the rest of the way to the van and fell against it, catching his breath. The entire cabin had been crushed, just as he'd thought. Fortunately, the cab was still intact, which meant he'd have access to the med kit and radio, if there was anyone out there to call.

He stepped around the front of the van cautiously, whisper-shouting Moore's name, not wanting to alert the creature on the roof of Puzzle House.

It was clear why she hadn't responded the moment he reached the sidewalk. A mess of blood, bone, innards and clothing lay in a ragged, wet heap in the walkway. If not for the uniform, he wouldn't have been able to tell what lay there was ever human. Moore's skull had been obliterated, splattered and smeared across the pavement. Her insides had been torn out, decorating the path like a maniac's game of hopscotch. The shotgun stuck out from an indeterminate body part, a flagpole marking her killer's territory.

Henry ran in a crouch toward it.

Likely alerted by his footfalls, the gallu shrieked and leaped off the roof. It dove, its heavy veined wings pounding, heading straight for Henry.

Certain he wouldn't make it, even if the shotgun was loaded, Henry scrabbled for the gun in his waistband. He caught it and jerked it free, raising it and firing one shot after another at the seemingly invincible creature hurtling toward him, until the clip was spent.

The gallu howled suddenly and dropped with a heavy thud at Henry's feet, curled up its wings, kicked out its clawed feet as it shuddered, and fell still.

Christ, this thing's almost as big as me!

The words he'd read from the Book came back to him, and he wondered how much of its prophecy had come true: *Lo, the mouth of the Watcher stretched wide across the firmament, and from the Great Beast's jaws came Legion....*

He looked up with a shudder, his mind reeling at the possibility. Could the stars still be up there, merely obscured by the eternally grinning maw of an ancient god so gargantuan it blocked out the sun, the moon and the stars, millions of gallu leaping from jaws lined with endless fathoms of razor-sharp teeth?

As if to prove him wrong, a cool raindrop struck his forehead. Suddenly it began to pour, pattering on the roof of the van and drenching the sidewalk. Henry laughed—but when he stuck out his tongue to catch a drop the laughter died in his throat with a retch at the taste of its salty, coppery tang. The liquid running down his arms was a viscous red.

Blood.

The sun disappeared from the sky, he thought, *and the Heavens rained with blood.*

Wasting no further time, Henry tucked the gun back into his blood-soaked waistband, hoping he'd come across more ammunition elsewhere, and rushed toward Moore's remains. He pulled the shotgun out by the barrel, the stock coming out with a sticky squelch, then searched the mess for her keys. He found them jutting out of what looked like a shattered hipbone, a broken cell phone and a heap of uncooked paté. He pulled them free, wiped them on his pants, and returned to the van.

While the rain of blood pattered down on the roof, it took him ten minutes to fish out the bullet and sew himself back up, sitting in the passenger seat with the door locked and the dome light on, intermittently checking the radio. No one returned his messages. Either the radio waves had been dampened like cell phone service inside the house, or there was nobody left alive to hear him. He chose to believe the former. It was best to think positively, even under the worst of circumstances. As far as circumstances went, he didn't think you could get much worse than this.

Patched up, Henry left the van during a break in the rain. Looking up from the sidewalk, he saw the door to Puzzle House swing open. Six dark figures stepped out one after another and gathered at the end of the walkway, standing motionless as department store mannequins. They weren't gallu—there were no wings, and they were distinctly male and female, standing upright. *Cultists?* he thought. As his eyes readjusted to the dark he recognized their faces, and the full realization of what completing the rituals in that house had accomplished struck him like a thunderbolt from Hell.

Six puzzles. Six sacrifices. Six demons.

Joy led the group, her head reattached to her neck with the sever clearly visible, eyeing him with a hideously malformed grin. Atkins and Ileana stood behind her, their own bodies reassembled. Rudy, Oscar and Jessica Danvers stood behind them. Each was naked, their eyes unblinking, the light mist of blood spattering their gray flesh.

Henry remained motionless in awestruck terror, unable to take his eyes off of them. Finally, the group broke apart, stalking off in opposing directions. Only Joy moved toward him. He backed up against the van as she neared, her eyes glowing with the same blue as the fire in the altar chamber.

She stopped at the foot of the walkway, cocking her head to one side, her bare toes curling over the edge of the pavement. Her skin glistened red in the guttering flames from the car down the street. Henry flinched as she reached out to him and gently caressed his cheek with the back of a hand.

"*Nungal welcomes you,*" she said, her lips unmoving, the voice rising from her lifeless throat not solely her own. It was as though two voices spoke to him. The second was deeper. Guttural. *Powerful.*

Joy's dead eyes regarded him a moment longer before she turned and began walking away, her bare feet making sticky sounds on the bloody pavement, her body moving sinuously, seductively toward the city.

It took all of his strength not to follow her.

Overhead, the gallu circled. Standing here any longer would just be waiting for another of them to come for him. It was time to get moving.

Guzzling from Atkins's water bottle, with pockets full of rattling shotgun shells, Henry left the house behind, staggering up Trap Street the way they'd come. He needed to find a phone, if any were left working. Mercy was out there somewhere, hopefully still alive, still safe. He wanted to call her and let her know he'd be home a little late.

He had a prize to collect first.

Whether it would be the money or their heads, he had yet to decide.

AL-QIYAMA CODEX
CHAPTER 51

[1]THE SUN DISAPPEARED FROM THE SKY [2]AND THE HEAVENS RAINED WITH BLOOD. [3]LO, THE MOUTH OF THE WATCHER STRETCHED WIDE ACROSS THE FIRMAMENT, [4]AND FROM THE GREAT BEAST'S JAWS CAME LEGION, [5]BRINGING WAR WITH THEM. [6]PESTILENCE AND FAMINE RODE UPON THEIR BACKS, [7]AND THE DISBELIEVERS WERE WASHED AWAY IN THE FLOOD.

A NOTE FROM THE AUTHOR

Congratulations! By finishing this book you have completed the mental rituals required to summon The Watcher, and usher forth His Thousand-Year Reign of Anguish and Misery— *huzzah!*

I kid. Or do I…? (Yes, I do.)

To say this book poured out of me would be like comparing the biblical flood to a light sprinkle. The introductory chapters eked out of me like sap from a tree, one drop at a time. But once our three main characters reached Puzzle House, this book came fast and furious, with the escape room puzzles, the demonology, myths and deaths piecing together as if by divine—or *not so divine*—intervention.

As always, I need to thank my wife, Sherri, for listening to my ideas as they were flowing out of me and still pretending to be surprised while she read it by plot points I'd told her weeks and months earlier. Thanks to my parents, who always nurtured my love of horror, even if they didn't share it, but particularly the tricks and scares I'd created for trick-or-treaters on Halloween night at the various houses we'd lived in.

Thanks to my good friend Danika Meyerson, who convinced me to research and outline the various traps, demons and gods almost immediately upon hearing the concept. I likely wouldn't have plowed through this story with as much enthusiasm, if not for her support and belief in this book before it was even a thing.

And thank *you*, dear reader, for picking up this book. Without you this is just words on the page. I raised the skeleton from the grave, but you dressed it up and made it dance.

I hope you consider leaving a review, positive, negative or somewhere in between, wherever you may have purchased it.

D.R. August 2023

ABOUT THE AUTHOR

Duncan Ralston was born in Toronto and raised in small-town Ontario, Canada.

Currently, he works in the television industry in Toronto, where he lives with his spouse.

He is the author of over a devil's dozen horror books, including the collections *Gristle & Bone, Video Nasties, In Every Dark Corner & Skin Flicks*, the novellas *Wildfire, Ebenezer* & the cult hit *Woom*, and the novels *Salvage, The Method,* the *Ghostland* Trilogy, *The Midwives & Gross Out*, and the gamebook *Try Not to Die: at Ghostland*, cowritten with Mark Tullius.

For 7 free short stories/novellas of dark fiction, signed bookplates, signed books and merch, please visit **www.duncanralston.com**.

THE MOVING HOUSE:
A PREQUEL TO

Winter, 2014

Long before it was called "Garrote House," superstitious neighbors had called it "the Moving House," though the house at 1 Hedgewood Crescent had stood unmoved at the end of the cul-de-sac, crooked and silent, for over a hundred and twenty years. From the outside it had a certain charm—it was the sort of house realtors might say had "good bones," but only if they were unfamiliar with its history. Because The Moving House had seen its share of bones… and flesh… and blood.

Christopher Hedgewood pulled the rented van up to the curb out front and peered out through the cracked passenger window at the darkened house. The house had been passed down to him through the generations, though it had seen its share of interlopers, each of whom had met an untimely and violent demise. Even his own ancestors hadn't been immune.

The house knew only violence. It *bred* it. Garrote House was his birthright. Both the Hedgewood family legacy and its curse.

"I've gotta be nuts," he told himself. Through a long sigh, he said it twice more. The seatbelt alarm dinged as he climbed out. The biting night air chilled his breath.

"You made it."

Christopher wheeled at the voice. Sara Jane Amblin stepped out of yet another new car. The streetlights at this end of the cul-de-sac had burned out. Backlit by the moon, his business partner had a sort of hazy glow like the female lead in an old black-and-white movie, her dark, high cheekbones shimmering. Christopher didn't much fancy women, but he knew a work of art when he saw one.

"I wouldn't dream of missing out," he said, hugging her briefly. Though the truth was he'd nearly not come at all.

Sara Jane looked up at the house, its gables like teeth gnawing at the black edge of midnight. "Shall we?" she said, holding out an arm for him to take.

He slipped his through hers, and felt her shiver through her puffy down-filled coat—more out of fright than the cold, he suspected. They gave each other challenging looks before starting toward the gate.

Stopping there, Christopher brought out his flashlight and shined it over the wrought iron arch. Rusted paint-flecked letters spelled out GARROTE HOUSE, entwined with the same sturdy Boston ivy—which still grew in Seattle, despite the name—smothering the low brick walls on either side of the walkway, and clawing its way up the front of the house to the windows on the second floor. Its dead leaves skittered along the cobblestones in the cold night air.

"This gate will have to come," Sara Jane said.

"I was just thinking that."

Relying on each other's courage, they passed under it arm-in-arm.

The Moving House didn't so much move as shift, and then only in subtle variations. Sara Jane's people had taken measurements in fifteen-minute intervals throughout the day, confirming that the interior walls would widen and narrow, widen and narrow again—almost as if the house itself were breathing. This movement was undetectable by the naked eye, but through the course of a day, the sofa, for instance, could be several inches from the window, and hours later butted up against it. The effect on the occupant was general uneasiness, a sense that something was not quite right, and whether it was this effect that had driven the house's occupants to madness was anyone's guess.

1 Hedgewood—the street named after the man who'd built the house, Christopher's great-great-grandfather Oliver Hedgewood, when it was the only house for miles—was what realtors would call a "stigmatized property." Over the years it had seen its share of tragedies: the usual deaths and injuries during construction, when such things happened regularly, the tuberculosis outbreak of the early 1900s, several suicides, homicides, and very few deaths stemming from old age. It was suggested by some to be a "sick building," a structure itself which caused illness as if by accident of shape and fate. But the final blow to its reputation was

when it entered the public's consciousness as a "murder house."

Clayton Odell had been a sculptor with a reputation for challenging established conventions. Considered by some to be "a modern Picasso," his art, particularly his sculptures, sold well enough to purchase the house at 1 Hedgewood in the late-'70s at a then-whopping $1.8-million. Odell's ironworks were monstrous caricatures of human invention throughout the ages. His Man and Machine, merging da Vinci's *Vitruvian Man* with his *Aerial Screw*, had stood in the lobby of the Metropolitan Museum of Modern Art for several years. It might have stood there today had the artist not made his final project the murder-suicide of his entire family in the summer of 1979. Odell's estate sold off his work and belongings. Sitting on prime Seattle land, the writer Rex Garrote—now also deceased—had snatched 1 Hedgewood up after a string of successful horror novels. Christopher had never had much interest in Garrote's books. The covers made them seem lurid, and even though his ancestors' house had seemingly inspired a trilogy of novels, Christopher still couldn't bring himself to read them.

He felt it would be like reading his family's history through the lens of a man obsessed with serial killers and monsters.

Garrote himself suffered a particularly gruesome death. The police believed it was self-immolation, though Christopher—who'd been a child at the time it happened—seemed to recall a detective suggesting the author wasn't dead at all, was merely in hiding. It would explain why no one who'd been in the house in the interim years had seen his ghost, many despite claims of seeing the others: the Odells, several builders, the house staff, and much of the long line of Hedgewoods leading all the way back to Ollie in the early 1900s.

Christopher didn't think it was likely, anyhow. How would a man with his level of fame—he'd had a TV show, after all, though it had only run for a year—have kept hidden for over a decade and a half? No, more likely that the house had claimed another victim. That she'd fed upon him psychically until she could finally feast on his physical self, as she had the rest.

After the horror writer's death, Christopher's father, August Hedgewood, purchased his family's former estate for a song and seemingly on a whim, with no real plans for the property. In the following years the house remained empty, falling into disrepair.

Christopher Hedgewood had been fascinated with houses since a very young age. His father—whom he loved but could not stand, and who likely shared the sentiment about his son—had no appreciation for architecture, only money. It wasn't until his early twenties that Christopher discovered the Garrote house was a part of his father's estate. Like his father, he'd had no idea what to do with it, only that he wanted it to be his.

In the years since the horror author burned himself to ash, neighbors reported hearing noises from inside, seeing strange lights. Ghouls obsessed with murder and a quick shot to fame broke in from time to time and came out terrified, banging on doors down the block, raving about becoming lost in a maze, asking startled occupants if they could see them. If they weren't, in fact, dead.

Just last year, a group of teenagers were interviewed

on the local news after the disappearance of their friend, claiming the young girl hadn't been kidnapped, as was believed by police, but had ventured into the Moving House alone and never come out.

Christopher had put a guard on the premises, worried there might be another incident. While genuinely concerned for safety, the same ambition that flowed through the blood of his ancestors burned in his, and he felt secretly happy for the unpaid publicity. By the time Jennifer Lynn Daniels went missing in 2009, Christopher had already begun toying with the kernel of an idea. If so many people wanted to enter the Moving House despite the reported dangers, why not give them what they wanted? An authentic, yet safe, haunting experience.

It wasn't until he met inventor and parapsychologist Sara Jane Amblin that Christopher decided it was possible. With all the strides she'd made in paranormal science during her work with the Hedgewood Foundation, Ms. Amblin was certain that with proper funding, she could provide him exactly the sort of experience he desired.

As it turned out, they'd already been working on that very thing—with Garrote's estate as a silent partner. It had been Garrote's idea to construct a haunting-themed amusement park, one filled with haunted buildings and objects he'd apparently been collecting throughout his life. It was Christopher's idea to thrust Garrote's posthumous involvement to the forefront, to use the writer's infamy among horror fanatics as a selling feature.

He was sure the psycho would have approved.

"What the general population thinks of as 'ghosts' are essentially energy imprints," Sara Jane had told him during their initial meeting. "They're echoes. The detection equipment I've designed for Hedgewood works the same way as a crime scene lamp illuminates trace evidence, after a fashion. What you see is the *imprint* of past life, like footprints left in the sand. When combined with my Recurrence Field, those echoes, those *imprints*, could theoretically last forever." Her dark eyes lighted. "Like photographs. Like moving photographs."

"This Recurrence Field," Christopher had asked, "you've seen it work?"

Back then the answer had disappointed him. In 2011, the Recurrence Field had been still a theory, though much closer to reality with Hedgewood's newfound understanding of what Sara Jane often referred to as "spiritual imprints."

"When you're dead you're dead," she explained. "That's the end of it. What I'm giving you is not life after death, but energy *beyond* death."

Naturally, Christopher was skeptical. Encoded in his DNA was the legacy of his third great-grandfather, legendary American showman John Purdy Hedgewood, proprietor of Hedgewood & Son Circus and father of Oliver, who'd built this house. The man had known how to spot a sucker, and how to prevent oneself from becoming one. Sara Jane had obliged Christopher's doubts with a demonstration.

"Was that window there before?"

Her voice startled him from his thoughts. Still approaching the house, she was looking up at a second-floor window, fear in her eyes, her breathing hurried. He followed her gaze. In the years since he'd discovered his father owned the Moving House he'd come here dozens of times: watching her, studying her. He knew every inch of her brick and mortar surface, of her wraparound porch, her gables, her hedges. He knew immediately Sara Jane was right. The octagonal window, each pane a stained-glass pastoral scene, had shifted a good three feet to the right, so it no longer rested below the middlemost gable. This phenomenon had never been recorded, only reported. The interior walls were constantly moving, but the exterior had always remained fixed to the same dimensions. Impossible... but the proof was there, before their eyes.

Her claws were already outstretched, burrowing into their minds like the twisted ivy clinging to her facade.

"It's a trick," he said. "She wants us to stay out."

"She?"

"All houses are female," he said. "Especially the crazy ones."

Sara Jane narrowed her eyes. "You've never gone inside at night, have you?"

Christopher shook his head.

"Are you sure you're ready?"

I've gotta be nuts, he thought again, and remembered the sweet elderly lady ironing her husband's shirts in the moment before the man stepped in with a shotgun and splattered her brains across the clean kitchen. Christopher had watched her eyes widen in horror again and again in the little post-war bungalow in Detroit, courtesy of Sara Jane's Recurrence Field. He saw the back of her head splinter, her blood and gray matter soil the fresh laundry—then a stutter as the scene "reset"—her shock, her fragmented skull, her blood—*stutter*—shock, skull, blood. On the fourth repetition his guts twisted in knots, and he'd run to the cramped bathroom to vomit. When he returned to the kitchen, the woman and her visible insides were gone. Sara Jane had turned off the Recurrence Field, apologizing.

"It never gets easier," she'd told him, though the emotion connected to the words had not been evident in her expression. Her expression had remained guarded as she packed away the heavy equipment. He'd helped her, eyeing her with suspicion.

"I'm ready," he said now. A sigh plumed from his lips as they stood on the creaking porch of the Moving House, where many a Hedgewood had lost their life.

He put the key in the lock and twisted it. The double doors swung inward with a gasp of musty air. He and Sara Jane shared a fearful look, then stepped across the threshold together.

Inside, blackout curtains covered the windows. Even the octagonal skylight in the rotunda's ceiling was covered. A double staircase wound its way up to the second floor on either side of a verde antique marble floor. Their flashlights skittered over disorienting patterns of white veins in the green serpentine stone. Having stood here hundreds of times in the dazzling light of day, neither Sara Jane nor Christopher marveled at its moldering beauty.

"Where should we start?" he wondered aloud.

"In the master bedroom. Where *he* started."

Sara Jane and her people had thoroughly researched the Moving House Murders from virtually every angle. Odell had begun in the workshop, grabbing up his tools. He'd begun in the middle of the night, while his wife Laura and their two children slept. Placing a hand over

Laura's nose and mouth—blood-spatter evidence had confirmed this long before the Recurrence Field would prove it—Odell stabbed his wife sixteen times in the heart, leaving nothing but bloody pulp.

Cries arose from the nursery next door. The boy had awakened to his mother's screams. Odell's bare feet left tacky red prints on the shiny hardwood until Laura's blood had dried, on his way to the nursery.

He entered the room, moving like a sleepwalker, arms hung loose at his sides, the chisel dripping blood on a shaggy, cow-shaped rug. He plodded over to his son's crib. Without a moment's hesitation, his arm rose and fell three times. The cries stopped abruptly. He did the same to his daughter, the boy's twin. He left the chisel in her tiny chest, carried her lifeless body like a skewered roast to the octagonal library at the epicenter of the house, laid it down then went back for the others. Once the entire family was reunited, Sam Odell set about taking them apart piece by piece with his sculpting tools: a hacksaw, an acetylene torch, the chisel.

Once he had finished, he sat surrounded by the severed body parts of his wife and children. His eyes and teeth gleamed white amid the glistening red of their blood drenching him from head to toe as he laughed.

And then he began to sew.

Christopher and Sara Jane ascended the stairs, fully aware of what awaited them on the floor above. She'd played back the scene a dozen times or more, following Odell from room to room on his brutal rampage… and not once did it ever get easier. Christopher had never desensitized to it, as he assumed he should. The sorrow was always as deep as the first time. He began to wonder if he'd made the right decision, if he should have used his influence on the chairs and shareholders to stop this thing before it went too far. This was his gift to the world: proof of life after death. Life *beyond* death. But he worried he might be following in the ill-fated footsteps of his late third great-grandfather, Purdy. He worried it was too late to turn back.

I've gotta be crazy, he thought, rising the stairs. *Go back, Christopher. Go home. Gregory's waiting. Our bed is warm. There's love there—not death. This is madness.*

They aren't real, Sara Jane's words on the phone tonight echoed in his mind, reassuring him after he'd expressed his concerns. *They feel nothing.*

He sometimes wondered if Sara Jane felt anything, if her dedication to scientific discovery hadn't smothered some of her humanity. She was a good woman: intelligent, a caring friend, responsible. But empathy seemed difficult for her. Christopher often thought she might be on the spectrum, though he had no proof of it.

The equipment was already set up on the second-floor landing: a series of large, smooth plastic machines with rounded edges, heavy and sanitary looking, like MRIs or CAT scanners. Christopher started the generator. Within seconds its thunderous sputtering began to echo throughout the house.

Sara Jane flicked a switch on the larger machine. It powered on with a high-pitched whine, flooding the hall with unnatural white light.

Once again, they put on their clunky, heavy helmets, prototypes for the AR glasses which were in the development stage now.

Footprints illuminated, the dull pink of echoed blood,

the bare feet padded down the hall hardwood from the master bedroom toward the twins' room as Clayton Odell—still hidden beyond the veil of death—staggered from the first murder to the second.

When the footprints reached the doorway, the man himself shimmered into existence: wispy at first, like a hologram, but as his semitransparent, bluish hand grasped the handle it appeared to solidify. It was not solid. Christopher had made certain of this during his initial experience with Odell, by stepping into the scene to grab the killer's arm, attempting to stop him from obliterating Laura Odell's heart. His hand had slipped right through Odell as though passing through a fog.

Odell's sleepwalker eyes stared into the middle distance as he opened the door. Sara Jane followed, skirting the footprints. Christopher stayed with the machine. Its protected cables ran along the wainscoting and into the master bedroom, continuing into the nursery, and down the next hall to the heart of the house, where Odell would soon spray his blood over the books lining the library walls.

"Where did he go?" Sara Jane said from behind the door.

"What?"

"Odell," she said, stepping out. Her expression betrayed none of the confusion or fear present in her voice. "He just disappeared."

"That's impossible," Christopher said. "Isn't it?"

"Impossible or not, he's gone."

Christopher met her at the doorway. Sure enough, the echo of Clayton Odell was nowhere in sight. Sara Jane pushed past, hurrying toward the hall. Christopher hung back in the doorway, watching young Adrienne Odell and her brother Aiden sleep peacefully—had the loop reset? He didn't know. He followed Sara Jane back into the hall.

She kept walking faster, faster, peering into open doors as she passed, following the cables down the hall, muttering "Fuck, fuck, fuck," as she went. Christopher kept pace behind her, looking through the same open doorways she had. They rounded a corner. A single lamp illuminated the hall, throwing their long shadows ahead of them.

"We should have turned on the overheads," Christopher said.

Sara Jane ignored him, but he knew how she would have answered: supplementary light rendered the detection lamps useless. Without them, the helmets they wore could not pick up the dead energy left behind. It was the same reason they'd covered the windows.

Out in the rotunda, the generator sputtered and the light behind them began flickering. Suddenly the house became silent. One by one, the large lamps extinguished, plunging them into a darkness so complete it was as if they had stepped off the edge of the universe.

"Christopher…?"

"I'm here."

"Don't move. I'm coming back."

Christopher remembered his flashlight. He flicked the switch. It came on weakly before winking out. "My flashlight won't work!"

"The Recurrence Field saps electricity from batteries within the field, remember? It works with energy."

He remembered—not that it had ever been a concern

during their daylight visits. He tucked the useless thing back into his coat pocket. Blood thundered in his eardrums as he waited for her hands to reach him. As the seconds stretched out, he began to worry the hands that would eventually grab him would not be hers. His muscles tensed. The hair on his neck stood up.

"*Sara...?*"

Not even the gentle swish of a hand brushing the wall met his ears.

"Sara! Where are you?"

Her voice called back from a distance, "I'm almost there!" A brief pause. "Did you move?"

"I've been standing right here! Where are you?"

"I guess I must have got turned around. I'll come back. Keep talking, okay?"

He couldn't think. His breathing grew panicked. "I don't know what to say," he shouted back.

"Then sing!"

Christopher racked his brain. Strangely, what came to mind was a song his mother had often sung to them as a lullaby, as it was one of few she knew by heart. He thought of her clear voice singing to his little brother in the crib when they were both young, a hand over her heart, and he called out, "'O beautiful for spacious skies—'"

"Really?"

"Do you want me to sing or not?"

"Keep going then." She sounded closer now.

"'For amber waves of grain, for purple mountain majesties, above the fruited plain!'"

His voice arose less tuneful than frantic. The windows rattled. He reached out to the wall, grounding himself, tethering himself to his rapidly diminishing grasp on reality. He thought of Odell, sitting cross-legged amid a spiraling tower of dusty old tomes, dragging the hacksaw teeth across his throat. "I don't want to sing this anymore."

"I'm almost there, keep going!" But her voice sounded even further away.

Christopher sang faster, blood racing: "'America! America! God shed His grace on thee! And crown thy good with brotherhood, from sea to shining—!'"

The silence drew out. He felt suddenly, inescapably alone.

"...*Sara?*"

A sconce flickered on near his head. The leap from pitch dark to sudden brightness startled him, though not so much as the presence before him. The nearly nude creature stood eight feet tall, a totem pole of warped human anatomy, a smooth-skinned man wearing the upper half of a woman on his shoulders, the once-pretty raven-haired head lolling left and right, its lips curled in a rictus. Two smaller pairs of arms hung loose, raggedly sewn to the man's sides like a macabre human octopus. Two piercing dark eyes stared out from the wet, crimson hole between the Odells's wailing children.

Christopher had a single moment to wonder how he'd managed to be in the library when he hadn't moved a muscle since the lights went out. Then the Odell Family snatched out with its many arms, grabbing him by the throat, the shirt, his abdomen. As the air escaped him, he heard Sara Jane call out his name from an impossible distance away.

He wanted to shout to her *Stay away*. He wanted to

tell her, *Turn back,* to tell her they'd made a mistake—all of it was a mistake from the very beginning. But the hands at his throat choked his words, and the world itself grew dim, until all he could see were the vacant eyes of a dead man, staring out from a jagged hole between two mounds of rotting flesh.

When the lights flickered on Sara Jane found herself standing above the stairs, barely an inch from what would have been a very bad fall. She stepped back hastily with a sharp inhale, marveling at how close to death she'd come. It would have been bitter irony to die here after all her work, in the house that inspired it.

It took her several minutes to find Christopher. By then rigor mortis had already begun to set in. She closed his eyes gently, and his mouth. His mask of terror was too much for her to bear. Though he had come here many times of his own volition, she felt some amount of personal responsibility. It was her work that had led to his death, after all. But whatever had happened to him, she was certain Christopher would want her work to continue.

With her cell battery close to drained, she placed a call to the Hedgewood Foundation. Someone would have his body moved off the premises. They would make it look like he died of natural causes, or suicide, or asphyxiation. No one would tie his death to this house, just one more in a long line of them, many from Christopher's own lineage.

The house had fed. Hopefully, it would not need to feed again for some time.

Very soon now, the Moving House would be literally